From: Delphi@oracle.org
To: C_Evans@athena.edu
Re: Arachne's child

Christine,

I think we've found another one of Jackie Cavanaugh's offspring. I hesitate to call her Jackie's daughter. After all, Jackie only provided the egg and the funds for genetic experimentation. As far as we know, Jackie never even visited her three children, much less provided any emotional support.

This woman has received a package that we've tracked to the remote hills of India. We know next to nothing about her, but I'm betting she has *enhancements*. Her sibling in Hong Kong was a genius trapped in an immobile body. Who can guess what curses—or gifts—this other child might have?

I'm putting all of our research resources into finding this woman—and any sisters she has left. If she's anything like her mother, we don't want her to get her hands on any of the information Jackie accumulated over the years.

I'll be in touch when we know more.

D.

Dear Reader,

I'm super excited about the release of *Untouchable* for two reasons. One, being asked to write an Athena Force book was like being asked to write for my favorite television show. As a fan of the first Athena Force series I was honored to be part of such a fabulous continuity. Then there was the added bonus of getting a pretty detailed preview of what was coming next. I go crazy for spoilers. I can't help myself.

Two, I've always wanted to write a heroine with superpowers. It goes back to my Wonder Woman days. Who didn't want those gold bracelets? When I learned that my heroine's special gift was poisonous skin I knew it was going to be a challenge, but I couldn't wait to dive in. I hope you have as much fun reading this story as I did writing it. It goes without saying I would love to hear what you think. You can visit me at www.stephaniedoyle.net

Stephanie Doyle

Stephanie Doyle
UNTOUCHABLE

ATHENA FORCE
Published by Silhouette Books
America's Publisher of Contemporary Romance

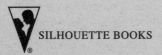

SILHOUETTE BOOKS

ISBN-13: 978-0-373-38982-7
ISBN-10:   0-373-38982-5

UNTOUCHABLE

Visit Athena Force at www.eHarlequin.com

Printed in U.S.A.

STEPHANIE DOYLE,

a dedicated traveler, has climbed Croagh Patrick in Ireland, snow-shoed on Mt. Rainier, crawled through ancient kivas of the Anasazi and walked among the blue-footed boobies of the Galapagos Islands. A firm believer that great adventures can lead to great stories, she continues to seek new challenges that will trigger her next idea. Readers can find out more about Stephanie by visiting her Web site, www.stephaniedoyle.net.

To my brother Pat,
who, like my heroine, lives in a foreign land.

Can't wait to visit.

Chapter 1

"Lilith! You must come quickly. Lilith!"

The sound of her name penetrated her sleep. She focused on the language that was being used. English. Not Hindi. One of the nuns rather than a villager. Slowly she opened her eyes and turned her head toward the noise. The heavy tarp that served as the door to her hut was pulled back. Sister Joseph filled the space.

"They are asking for you on the hill. You must hurry."

The plump older woman stepped inside and instantly Lilith pushed herself farther back on her sleeping mat. "Do not get too close. I am not dressed."

The sister obeyed and turned away. Lilith got out of bed and began to assemble what had become her unique habit. First, a cotton slip. Then, a long bolt of silk she pulled over her head that covered her from neck to foot, shoulder to wrist. Ties secured the material to her body, making the uniform less cumbersome. At times she was sure she must be mistaken for a mummy.

Finally she reached for the gloves that sat on her writing table, which was the only other piece of furniture in the small hut other than her sleeping mat. As she slid the gloves up her arms Lilith felt the material cling to her skin. It was a sensual feeling that she allowed herself to enjoy for only a second.

"The brothers have need of your…medicine," Sister Joseph told her with her back still turned to her. The brothers were Buddhist monks rather than Christian brothers, but the nuns who lived in the village situated below the monastery treated them with as much reverence.

"They have a visitor among them. Looking for retreat, I think. I believe a leg wound has festered."

"Leprosy?" Lilith asked. "Has he become infected by one of the villagers?"

"No." Sister Joseph shook her head. "He hasn't been exposed to anyone long enough. Unless he contracted it somewhere else. Listen to us," she said sheepishly. "A man comes in with a wound and we automatically assume it is one of the rarest and hardest-to-contract diseases in the world. We're growing paranoid I think."

"But this is our world," Lilith reminded her. "It is what we see every day. It is natural to make assumptions. I will go to the brothers. I'll see what can be done."

The woman backed out of the hut and Lilith followed her at a distance. It was still night, but nearing morning. Animals in the forest just beyond the village sent signals to their comrades to start the day. They were familiar sounds but still exotic to Lilith's ears even after all this time.

She followed the path that led from her camp up a steep hill that was flattened at the top. A hundred years ago devout monks had come together to build a monastery as a tribute to Buddha. Today it served the same purpose.

Deep in the region of Arunachal Pradesh, near the China border, this track of forest was almost forgotten to the rest of India. As were her human inhabitants. It was why the monks had claimed this space in their search for solitude. It was why the lepers had been banished here, ejected from society.

It was why Lilith called it home.

The trail steepened noticeably but Lilith didn't falter, her legs well used to the path. Although she chose to live among the Christian nuns who had come to care for the lepers, it was the monks with whom she continued her spiritual education. Poor Sister Joseph tried so faithfully to convert Lilith. But while she enjoyed the stories of the man known as Jesus, for in many ways he was also an outcast from his people, there was something about the monks' teachings that called to her.

Maybe because she was surrounded by so much death. The idea of coming back to life to try again appealed to her. Obviously there was more to the religion and Lilith embraced all facets of it, but it was the idea of returning as something different, someone different, that mattered to her.

Not that she ever planned to tell Sister Joseph. The woman would be crushed if she knew there was no hope for conversion. Still, despite their varying religious beliefs, the monks and the nuns had no problem coexisting. If neither subscribed to the other's beliefs they still respected the sacrifice each had made for their faith.

As she climbed higher, the air thinned. Lilith could see the structure in the dark. The monastery was built of stone and mud bricks. An impressive sight, it rose three stories and had over a hundred different rooms linked by long corridors. It was a square design with an orchid garden in the center that Lilith knew the monks referred to as the inner sanctum.

At the main entrance Lilith pulled down hard on a rope several times to announce her presence. The bell clang could be heard throughout the compound.

Eventually the door opened and beyond it she recognized Tenzig, one of the younger brothers. His head was shaved and he was wrapped in the traditional saffron-colored robe that declared his spiritual path. His expression was as serene as ever. He stepped back to allow Lilith to enter, clearly not surprised by her arrival and not in any particular rush. They spoke in the hushed tones of his language as he directed her through the labyrinth of hallways.

"Tell me again, why am I here?" Not that she didn't trust Sister Joseph's version of events, but she found herself needing the distraction of conversation. There was always risk involved when her medicine was needed. It made her nervous. She could feel her heart racing just thinking about what needed to be done.

"A visitor came to us. Looking for peace. He walked with a limp. Now the fever has taken him and we fear the only recourse is to remove the leg. He needs to… sleep…before we can do this. You understand?"

"Sister Peter has seen him?"

"She is already with him. We went to her first."

Sister Peter had recently arrived from the United States. A medical-school dropout who had been called by her faith to take a different path, she had quickly proven herself an invaluable asset among the monks, the nuns and the villagers. If Sister Peter was concerned the leg would have to come off, then the situation was as grave as Tenzig said.

"You can't take him to a town? Find a real doctor?" Lilith could only imagine the shock the man would suffer to be put to sleep against his will only to wake and find a leg missing.

"There is no time and it is too far to travel even by automobile. Also, we think he would not want to leave this place. We think he would not want the exposure that his wound might cause in a village large enough to have a hospital."

Lilith nodded. Many who came to the monastery who claimed to be searching for peace were actually looking to get lost. This man, it seemed, was no exception. A criminal maybe. Dangerous possibly. Perhaps she would serve a greater good by giving him more than a numbing sleep. It would be so easy. A simple touch.

If only death weren't so very disgusting to her.

They stopped beside a door and Tenzig knocked gently. He was commanded to enter. Inside the room Lilith saw another brother, Punab, sitting side by side with Sister Peter as the two of them tended to the man on the bed.

The patient was naked but for a cloth that had been draped over his hips, no doubt in deference to the sister's sensibilities. His hair was thick and ink-black. Damp, too, from either the fever or the cold compresses being applied.

His chest was broad, well defined with muscle and covered with the same inky-black hair as what was on his head. His legs, too, looked thick. Strong. It was as if he exuded strength despite the flush of fever on his cheeks. There was a heaviness to the man without being fat. A solidness that his entire body conveyed. Even in his hands and his feet.

Lilith wondered how much his body matched his spirit. If they were at all close, she predicted he would be stubborn. It would not be easy to kill this man. Certainly it would take more than a mere fever.

Glancing over the rest of his body, she saw, high on the inside of his left thigh, the infected injury. Almost perfectly round, it was viciously red and oozing pink puss.

Definitely a bullet wound. Lilith had seen enough of them when hunters poaching tigers had missed their mark and found people instead.

"I can't get his fever down. And he won't let us get close enough to the wound to see what's causing the infection," Sister Peter relayed.

Lilith could see the concern on the woman's face. Her dedication was unquestionable, but she was not a doctor. She would feel responsible if something happened to him in her care even knowing that she had done everything she could. If for no other reason, Lilith wanted to help her friend. She would do what was asked of her regardless of the risk.

"He won't *let* you?" Lilith asked. "He is weak from fever. Can't Punab and Tenzig hold him down?"

Both monks were smaller than the man on the bed and more used to meditation and study than fighting, but surely in this man's weakened condition the two of them could subdue him.

Punab, much older than his sister counterpart, a fact emphasized by his deeply lined face, shook his head. "This man is not like others. This man is…a warrior. He'll not be held unless he chooses."

Lilith translated the monk's words since she knew Sister Peter still hadn't grasped the nuances of Hindi.

"A warrior, huh? More likely a thief who got caught on the run. We've seen his kind come to the monastery before. They say they're looking for enlightenment then after a few days, when they figure the coast is clear, they disappear. No doubt this one would have done the same if he hadn't gotten sick."

He didn't look like a thief, Lilith thought. Something about his jaw, the shape of it, made him seem too proud. He was Indian—she could determine that by the bronze color of his skin—but his features had been sharpened by another race. She watched him for a long minute and decided that while he was not a thief, she could not say for certain that he wasn't a killer.

Warriors killed, after all.

Suddenly his eyes popped open and he focused on her. "Don't let them take my leg."

Startled by his sudden alertness, Lilith took a step back. He spoke in English and his accent was British.

"You need to rest," she replied in his language. "I can help you sleep. I can take the pain away."

"No," he rasped. "They'll take it while I sleep. You can't let them."

Lilith moved closer to the bed. Impulsively she reached out to him, thinking to adjust the damp cloth on his head and soothe it over his face to remove the droplets of sweat that beaded his forehead. But she caught herself before she touched him.

It wasn't in her nature to touch anyone. For comfort or anything else. Even when she was wearing her gloves. But clearly the man needed to be assured. What Lilith didn't know was if her assurance would be a lie.

She met Sister Peter's steady gaze. The two women were a stark contrast to each other. The nun's blond hair to Lilith's dark. Sister Peter's brown eyes to her gray. Tall where Lilith was not. But despite their physical, religious and cultural differences they communicated easily and without many words.

"I can try. No doubt something was left inside the wound. A bit of dirt or debris. I can try to cut around it and clean it out. But if the infection worsens…"

There was no need to finish the thought. It was a common misassumption that leprosy somehow caused limbs to simply fall off a person's body. The truth was that the numbness caused by nerve damage often resulted in minor cuts left untreated for too long. In the heat and humidity, infection would take hold quickly, leaving amputation as the only recourse.

Lilith had been witness to the procedure too many times since she'd arrived here from Nepal. Glancing down again at the man on the bed, she found it hard to imagine how he would handle the loss of his limb. Clearly the fear of it was enough to keep him fighting through the delirium of fever.

"Let us see what we can do. After all, it is such a nice leg." Lilith smiled softly and Sister Peter smiled back. Tenzig and Punab made no comment.

"The cup, Tenzig." Lilith pointed to a shelf that held a clay cup used for transferring water out of a larger bowl in the room that was continually kept filled. Cleanliness was serious business for the monks and they spent nothing short of an hour every day rinsing their bodies and their spirits of dirt.

Carefully Lilith tugged at the material bunched at her fingers until the glove slipped off. She started to reach for the cup that Tenzig filled when she saw him freeze.

She might have thought that it was fear of her that had him rooted to the floor, if she hadn't seen the quick glance he gave toward the bed. Lilith heard the gasp of Sister Peter before she actually felt the grip of a hand around her left wrist.

The man's grip was tight but it was clear his intention wasn't to hurt her. Merely to get her attention.

He had it.

Her eyes were pinned to where his hand circled her delicate wrist less than an inch away from the exposed skin of her hand. "Let go," she said softly.

"You can't let them do it," he said. "You can't let them cut it off. No matter what happens…you can't. I must be able to run. I have to run…."

Lilith looked away from where he was holding her and focused on his flushed face. "I won't let them take it. You will run again. You will see. But you need to let me go."

He said nothing. His chocolate eyes remained fixed on hers.

She tried to smile gently the way she thought a mother might smile to give ease and comfort to a sick child. "It is going to be all right. I won't let them hurt you. Let go now."

"Your face…" he whispered then swallowed hard.

Lilith's brow furrowed. He couldn't know her. She was sure that she had never seen his face before. She would have remembered.

"Your skin…so…beautiful."

He used his free hand to reach for her, his finger outstretched almost as if he intended to caress her cheek. Lilith pulled her body away from his outstretched hand. Eventually his lack of strength defeated him and his hand fell back to his side. Feeling his grip loosen, she tugged slightly and that arm also fell back against his stomach.

"Quickly, before he moves again."

Tenzig jumped forward and held the cup out to her. Lilith took it with her gloved hand. She closed her eyes and took several deep breaths.

Please, she thought. *Please don't let me hurt him. Please don't let it be too much.*

She dipped a single finger into the cup of water and circled the rim once. Then, because of his size, once more. She handed the cup back to Tenzig.

"Start with a few sips first," she warned Sister Peter. "See how he reacts to it. If while you're working he moves or starts to revive just a brush on his lips will work. Remember not to let it touch your skin. What you do not use must be poured out into the ground not mixed with any other water source."

"I'll be careful."

Lilith nodded. She took a final glance at the man and saw that his eyes were closed but she doubted he slept peacefully. After a few sips that would change.

There was nothing left for her to do, but she found herself reluctant to leave him. It was probably irrational.

For a moment she felt as if her presence had meant something to him.

"I will do everything I can, but remember I'm no surgeon," Sister Peter warned. "I can't promise anything."

"I know you will do your best. That is all he can ask for. He is lucky that he has you in such a place. And if something should go wrong, you carry no guilt for your effort."

Despite her words, Lilith felt a quiet confidence that the nun would succeed. Not only was her faith in Sister Peter unquestionable, but the man's strength and determination was also a force to be reckoned with. Together she was sure they could beat back the infection and defeat the invasive fever.

Sensing that she had lingered too long already, Lilith pulled her attention away from the bed.

"If I am not needed anymore, I will head back to the village."

"Tenzig will walk you," Punab said. "Once again we are grateful to our sister. Our Sangha is lucky to have such a unique person in our midst."

Lilith bowed her head in response.

His words only served to remind her how unusual this small piece of earth was and how grateful she was to have found this place. There were very few communities that would be grateful to have someone like her in their midst. Like a leper, she was an outcast.

Unwanted.

Feared.

Tossed out like garbage, first by her mother's family, then by her father.

Lilith tried to forgive those who didn't understand. More, she attempted to see the decision through their eyes. There had been a reason why she had been rejected by her people and ultimately evicted from her home.

She was an agent of death.

Chapter 2

"How is he?" Lilith called out to her friend.

It had been almost a week since her midnight summons to the monastery and every day she thought about the warrior.

Sister Peter had spent the first two days and nights at the stranger's bedside doing everything she could to save his leg as well as his life. After a pitched battle with the raging fever it was finally acknowledged that the man was too stubborn to die. At least that was what Sister Peter told Lilith when she eventually returned to the village. She declared that not only would he live, but he would also keep the leg.

Stubborn, just as Lilith had suspected.

Since then the dedicated nun had visited him daily

to monitor his progress. Lilith wasn't sure if Sister Peter was merely doing her due diligence or if secretly she was taking satisfaction in a job well done. Hard work and success weren't praised by the other nuns.

It was expected.

Today she had gone again to check up on him and Lilith waited for her at the bottom of the hill as she had every day to hear news of his condition. She couldn't say why she would not go to the monastery to see him herself. She told Sister Peter it was because she did not want to risk another incident like the one that night, but now that the fever was gone she imagined she could avoid his touch without any explanation. Lilith's condition wasn't something she shared with passing strangers.

Each day she thought about it. Each day she waited for Sister Peter to deliver the news instead.

Slowly Sister Peter descended the steep path that led away from the monastery. Lilith could see the weariness on her face from the extra burden of his care, but mingled with the fatigue was the serenity that came from doing what she believed she'd been born to do.

Lilith almost envied her.

"He's doing better than yesterday," Sister Peter said. "Actually walking on the leg a little. Remarkable given his condition a week ago."

"No danger at all, then, that he will lose the leg?"

The sister stopped and shook her head, a faint smile on her face. "Not now, no. He's lucky I found that fragment of bullet left in the wound. Time should tell whether or not there's any lingering damage to the muscle, but he's young and strong. No reason to think he shouldn't be perfectly fine in a few weeks. I'm sure I'm imagining it, but I think the brothers were particularly grateful I didn't cut up their warrior. I can't tell if they fear him or revere him."

A warrior. That was what Punab had called him. However, they had also let him into their sanctuary. They let him stay to search for whatever it was he'd come looking for. There must be some trust there.

"That is good news," Lilith said. "Once again I do not know what we would do without your skills."

"I was thinking the same thing about you."

"Mine is not so much a skill, I think. However, I am grateful I did not kill him."

Sister Peter raised a single eyebrow, a trick that fascinated Lilith. "You seem awfully concerned with our new patient. You did hear me when I said I pulled a bullet fragment from his leg."

"I heard you. And I know how the wound was caused. I am not concerned for him. I am just…"

Lilith had no answer for how she felt. He was a strong man. A handsome man, too. She supposed if she had to be honest with her friend she would say that he attracted her on some level. Which was strange. She wouldn't have imagined that she could ever feel such an elemental connection with another person.

Attraction was useless to her. It had no hope.

It was one of the reasons she knew that although she

studied with the monks on the path to enlightenment she could never consider herself a Buddhist nun. To do so would mean practicing celibacy, one of the five precepts. For those on the path this meant sacrifice. For Lilith it meant survival.

Not that such a thing mattered. The title of nun had been lost to her long ago when she had broken the first precept: do no harm. She'd broken that precept many times.

Sister Peter often tried to convince Lilith that what she did to end suffering or what she did by accident could not be considered a sin. But dead was still dead to those she touched. Maybe it wasn't intentional, but it was a result of her actions. For that she knew she could never fully walk the path to true enlightenment. At least not in this lifetime.

There was, however, always the next.

"I am merely glad he lived," Lilith insisted. "That neither one of us was responsible for killing him."

Sister Peter smiled. "Amen."

A noise penetrated their conversation, forcing Lilith's head upward. She instantly identified the sound of machine rather than animal.

"Sounds like we are going to have more visitors."

"Hmm. It's been a while since she's been here," Sister Peter noted as she also studied the sky, waiting for the helicopter to catch up with the sound. "Several months. I thought maybe she was gone for good."

Lilith took in the sister's worrisome expression.

"That sounds more like wishful thinking on your part. Do you not like our benefactress?"

Sister Peter folded her arms over her chest and frowned. "It seems petty, doesn't it? After all, without her money we wouldn't be able to afford the multiple-drug therapy that's worked so well for those infected. Especially the children. But…"

"But?"

"There's something about her, Lilith. Don't you think it's odd the way she seems to be so fascinated by you?"

Lilith shrugged. She hadn't really considered it. It was clear to any newcomer that she was set apart from all the other groups. Not a nun or a monk or a villager. She imagined it was natural to be curious as to who she was, what role she served.

"I believe she thinks I am some kind of tribal healer. Of course, she does not understand how I make the medicine that I dispense."

"Doesn't she? The way she follows your every step when she's here. The questions she's always asking the sisters and the villagers about you. For a woman who is simply supposed to be doing good works with her money as she claims to be, her actions feel very… deliberate."

"She never stays for long," Lilith pointed out. "She will come and go and we will have that much more money as a result of her visit."

Together Lilith and Sister Peter headed back to the village. The incoming helicopter caused the uproar it normally did. The children, desperate for distraction from their monotonous days, ran to the clearing that had been carved out for supply drops.

Supplies and Jacquelyn Webb's helicopter.

A woman with apparently unlimited resources, Jackie owned the helicopter that flew her from Bomdila, the nearest city, into the heart of the jungle. A self-proclaimed philanthropist, she heard about the leper colony during a plea from the Franciscan nuns at her local church. Urged to act, she set up funds that allowed for a continual flow of the necessary medicines to treat leprosy in the tiny village. One day she decided that sending money wasn't enough. She needed to come and meet the people infected with the horrible disease in order to determine how else she could help.

That was the story she told Lilith on her first visit. At the time Lilith saw no reason to question the older woman's sincerity. However, now that Sister Peter had brought it to her attention she had to admit that Jackie very rarely showed any interest in the sick or even in the progress her money had made possible.

Instead her interest was in Lilith. How she'd come to be here. Why she'd chosen to stay. How she prepared the medicine that so many of those infected said took away the pain.

It was impossible to keep Lilith's condition from those she lived with; too many precautions were needed. Although the sisters had often tried to convince her to find medical treatment for what they called her disease, they never pressed the issue or discussed it with outsiders.

Despite her financial contributions, Jackie was an outsider.

When Jackie asked about her strange garb, Lilith played it off as a uniform chosen by some women practicing Buddhism. When Jackie offered to take her out of the village, to see some of the other sights of India, Lilith simply declined without explanation.

By the time they reached the landing site the children were crowded together to watch the show. As the helicopter began its descent into the thick foliage that threatened daily to overtake the man-made landing pod, they waved and danced about. Blades rotated so quickly it was nearly impossible to see them.

The helicopter's wheels touched down and Lilith saw that the pilot was the only passenger. Jackie hadn't come, but her helicopter had.

The pilot emerged from the machine. On his shoulder he carried a satchel, and after maneuvering his way through the children who were all pleading for rides, he spotted Lilith. He paused for a second to study her.

Finally he walked directly to her. "You're Lilith?"

Lilith took a step back. She didn't recognize his accent, but he wasn't Indian.

"I am."

"This is yours." He slipped the satchel's strap off his shoulder and lowered it carefully to the dirt in front of her feet. Then he stepped away and once again threaded his way through the clamoring children. He got back in the chopper and almost instantly he was lifting off from the jungle floor.

"What was that about?" Sister Peter asked as she came up behind Lilith.

"I have no idea." Kneeling, Lilith inspected the satchel. She flipped open a flap and pulled out another smaller black bag. Inside that she found a thin black square that she recognized. Jackie used to bring it with her every time she traveled. She said it was so she could stay connected to the outside world.

She showed it to Sister Peter.

"A laptop? She sent you her computer."

Lilith shrugged and then reached into the satchel again. This time she pulled out a small box and an envelope. She opened the box and pulled back when she saw a fat gold spider sitting on black velvet. Shaped like a black widow, it was incredibly detailed. Small head, thin, wiry legs and a two-inch-long round bottom. Despite it being a replica, Lilith could almost feel its deadly aura. Her fingers trembled as she touched it.

"Not exactly my taste in jewelry," Sister Peter noted. "Even if I hadn't taken a vow of poverty."

Lilith pulled it from the box and saw that the spider was attached to a gold chain. She looked at it quizzically.

"Do you think it was intended to be a gift?"

"Do you have a penchant for spiders?"

Lilith shuddered. "No. But it is heavy. If it is gold, it could be worth a great deal. Why would she send such

a thing? I have no need of personal money or posses-
sions. Only donations that can be used for the village.
Do you think she wants me to sell it? I cannot imagine
such a thing would be easy." She didn't want to verbal-
ize it, but the necklace was very ugly.

"Read the letter." Sister Peter pointed to the envelope
in Lilith's hand.

Having almost forgotten it, Lilith set the necklace
back in its case and tore into the envelope. It was written
in English, but Lilith had command of the written
language as much as she did the spoken one.

The key is in the spider. Use it wisely.
Welcome to your new life.
Jackie (A)

"Welcome to your new life...." Sister Peter read over
Lilith's shoulder. "What does she mean by that?"

"I do not know. The key is in the spider...."

Lilith scooped up the box and stood. She pulled out the
spider and studied it from all sides. Turning it on its back,
she spotted a seam in the gold. Using her thumb, she
pushed and pulled until the back slid open. Inside was a
small silver rectangular device that Lilith didn't recognize.

"I know what that is," Sister Peter said. "It's a
memory stick."

Lilith shook her head. "I do not know...."

"A flash drive. You insert this into the back of the
computer in one of the USB ports. It stores files. Like

a floppy disk or a CD only smaller and with more space. It means there is information on it. Information you can view if you plug it into the computer."

"I do not understand. Why would she send me computer files? Here? And the letter *A* next to her name. I thought her last name was Webb. None of this makes any sense."

"Then make sense of it. Read what's on the files. You've probably got a few hours of battery life on this laptop. That should give you enough time to sort through whatever it is she wanted you to have."

Lilith took the memory stick from Sister Peter and put it back into the spider's belly.

"I was supposed to go to the monastery for study this afternoon," she said absently. She had also thought that maybe today she would overcome whatever was holding her back and stop in to check on the visitor's condition. She'd wanted to see for herself that he was doing well and that his leg was getting better.

And if she were honest with herself, she wanted to talk to him without him being delirious this time. Given his improving condition, it seemed likely he would be leaving soon. This could be her last chance.

"I have to go back up in a few hours to check on your friend's bandages and to make sure he isn't pushing himself too hard. I'll let them know you've been detained."

"I feel anxious, though. Reading what is on this computer. What if it is private? What if this is a mistake and Jackie simply sent this ahead of her arrival?"

"If it was a mistake she wouldn't have written the note. And if it was that private she wouldn't have sent it to you at all."

"I know one thing for certain. I do not want a new life," Lilith said adamantly, referring to Jackie's message. "This is my life. I cannot imagine why she would write such a thing."

Sister Peter shook her head and smiled sadly. "Oh, Lilith, this isn't a life. This is an escape. Trust me, I know."

"That is not true." Lilith was stunned by the sister's words. "I am needed here. I contribute. I belong here."

"Of course you contribute. And yes, you are welcomed here. I didn't mean to imply that you weren't. Only that… Well, you didn't get to choose this place. It was chosen for you. You didn't get to decide what you wanted to do with your life. It was decided for you."

"Not decided," Lilith corrected her. "Dictated. Dictated by my condition. You have seen what I can do. I have no other choice."

"Yes, I've seen what you can do," she allowed. "But you don't know if your condition can be treated. You have never tried to leave this place to find out. Accept the truth. You were sent here as a punishment by your family. A punishment you didn't deserve because you couldn't possibly help what happened."

"I have never spoken of what happened," Lilith said quietly. "You do not know what I did."

"I know it must have been bad for your father to do what he did, but I also know you were a child. Barely thirteen when you were abandoned here. You stay in this place to punish yourself for this wrong you feel you've committed. That's not living life. That's suffering in purgatory."

Lilith recognized the word from Sister Joseph's many sermons. Purgatory was a place you went after death to atone for your sins before moving on to heaven.

Glancing around the village, she saw the small huts and so many of the thin, suffering bodies that filled them. There were good days here, but she couldn't deny that most of them were filled with pain. Pain she could only ease for a little while.

Maybe Sister Peter was right. Maybe this was purgatory.

But that didn't mean that Lilith didn't belong here.

Chapter 3

The screen turned black as she continued to press her finger down on the power button. Lilith wasn't sure if it was the proper way to stop the computer but it was the only thing she could think of to make the words go away. And she so desperately needed to make them go away.

If you're reading this I'm dead....

The awful part was that Jackie being dead was the least disturbing piece of information in her files.

Genetic experiments. A new breed of powerful women. My offspring. My daughters.

Shaking her head, Lilith tried to remove the flashes of phrases that were burned behind her eyes, but they wouldn't let go of her. She couldn't unread what she'd read or unlearn what she'd learned. It would be with her now. Always.

Surrogate mother…two others created of my eggs… each of you now has a piece of my empire… Put the pieces together and all will be revealed… This is a taste…

Hungry yet?

Hungry? A taste?

Empire.

That word stood out among the rest. It was the word Jackie used to describe the endless amounts of folders on her memory stick. Some of the folders were names. Names that even in the far reaches of Arunachal Pradesh Lilith recognized. Leaders of the world, who had lied, cheated, raped and killed. Sinners, all of them, who paid money to hide their crimes rather than admit their mistakes and be punished for them. Vaguely Lilith wondered if they hadn't simply created their own version of a lifelong purgatory.

And there was more. So many folders that she couldn't open, but after what she'd already read she couldn't imagine going any further. Couldn't conceive of wanting to know more than she did.

Closing the lid on the laptop, she stood and moved away from it. Lilith knew she would never be able to move as far away from the machine as she needed to be to forget. She didn't believe the world was that big.

Jackie Webb, Arachne as she'd referred to herself, was Lilith's biological mother. That had been in the first folder Lilith read. The documents indicated that the woman in whose womb she'd grown had been nothing more than an incubator for a genetic experiment. Had she known when she agreed to do this what they were putting inside her? Did she have a choice?

Did she ever suspect that the baby she was giving life to would ultimately poison and kill its host?

The impact of what this meant, of what she'd learned, was suddenly too much to handle. It was like having the secrets of the universe revealed all at once. Her mortal mind was too fragile to take it in. She needed to leave. She needed to find someplace where she could let the information settle in her head and in her heart.

The monastery. There she could clean herself. In the garden she could let the water rush over her body, taking away the filth she'd been exposed to. She would remember who she was—not what the computer had revealed but who she had become since her birth.

Lilith started for the opening to the hut but stopped. The computer sat on her writing table, so out of place in the stark space she'd called home for these last ten years. She could still feel the heat it gave off. Or was what she was feeling something more sinister? Part of her wanted to destroy the computer and the tiny piece of metal inside it. But she knew she couldn't. The information it contained was simply too important.

Walking back to it, she removed the stick from the back of the computer and found the spider necklace still nestled inside the box she'd place on her table. She turned it over and slid open the back, returning the flash drive to its hiding place. Leaving the necklace wasn't an option, but the thought of wearing it made her shudder.

She had no choice.

Lilith pulled the gold chain around her neck and fastened the catch in the back. Then she tucked the gold body inside her silk coverall where it rested against her skin, safe from another's touch.

Avoiding the greetings from the villagers and, more important, avoiding Sister Peter, who would have nothing but questions, she made her way up the steep hill to the monastery.

Another young monk answered the summons at the door. Pema had recently been sent to the monastery by his family in Nepal. If the beads of sweat that habitually formed on his shaved head were any indication, he still hadn't gotten used to the weighted heat.

Lilith spoke in a dialect native to his land, one that she remembered from her childhood in Nepal, and he smiled. Thinking she had come for study, he pointed to where she knew Punab typically held his classes, but instead she made for the inner courtyard fashioned with water pumps and basins where the monks did their bathing as well as their laundry.

Winding her way through the series of walkways, Lilith found the center of the building. The burst of color inside the garden was so comforting she could have wept. This was the place she came from. The place where she'd begun to learn who she was. Not that other place. Not some lab.

Carefully she reached out and touched the delicate petals of the orchids that flourished under the brothers' care. So much like her own skin, she thought. Soft and silklike with just a hint of dew. Sometimes others thought she glowed. It hadn't been a curse as her father believed. It wasn't a sickness like the nuns suggested.

What had been done to her had been done on purpose. By Jackie.

Frowning, Lilith let the flower fall from her hand and made her way deeper into the courtyard where she found a series of pumps. Taking a large clay bowl with a flat bottom that had been specifically designated for her use, she placed it under the pump and began to call up water from the well that resided under the brick building.

In deference to her sex, she sought out the three-sided partition that the brothers had constructed for her. It allowed her privacy during her bath as well as prevented the monks from being tempted by her femininity should they stumble upon her. Once behind it she felt free to unwrap the bindings that encased her.

Tarak winced. He felt the pinch in his thigh with every step he took and figured he was overdoing it, but he wouldn't let himself stop. In a sick way, he was happy to feel the pain. It reminded him that he had a leg. His fault, he told himself. When he'd arrived at the monastery's doorstep he hadn't been paying attention to the nagging pain in his thigh. Only the one in his soul.

Eventually the fever had overtaken him to the point

where he'd known he was in trouble. Spending more time in the jungle than most, he'd seen what fever unchecked by medicine could do to a man. A merciless thief, it could rob a man of his strength, then his sanity, until finally it took his life.

Lucky him, he'd been spared both his life and his sanity. Or had he?

Images still haunted him from that night when the monks had come to his room. It seemed otherworldly. Surely a sign that he'd lost his mind. There had been two women with Punab. A plain-faced one, simple and forthright. She'd wiped his brow and told him to hold on— that someone was coming to take away the pain. He'd felt the fire in his body. The heat was focused most intensely where the bullet had ripped through the flesh of his upper thigh.

He remembered lying in his sweat thinking that the heat was good. The pain was good. He deserved it. He'd earned it. Everyone else had died. But he had lived and for that he needed to suffer.

He wanted to tell the woman in the rumpled white habit that he craved the pain. Because not only was it punishment, it was proof. Proof that he was alive. That he'd been smarter than the enemy who had betrayed him. There was satisfaction in that even though his men were dead.

Where had it gone wrong?

Tarak stopped in his wanderings. He reached down to massage the muscles around the wound, working his fingers deep into his leg to ease the cramps. When he looked up, the colors of the garden exploded before his eyes and he realized he'd made it from his room to the center-court orchid garden.

He wanted to appreciate the beauty in front of him, but instead his mind kept working back to the question that had stayed with him every day since the incident.

How had he failed?

He could ignore the lingering questions. Accept what happened and move on. Tell himself that it was the job. The risk they all took. But he knew himself well enough to know he never would.

Instead he let himself think back to the specifics of the mission.

He took himself back to the compound outside of Monteria, Colombia. It wasn't hard. The sweet scent of the orchids reminded him of another jungle on the other side of the ocean.

Back there it had been darker and the stench almost rancid. The rain hadn't just fallen on their heads, it had cascaded. But they all knew the job, and rain wasn't something they let get in the way. Six soldiers. All contracted by the CIA. Tarak had been chosen to lead.

Mistake number one, he thought grimly. He'd allowed the CIA to pick some of the team rather than do it himself. The soldier-of-fortune community was a relatively small one. In the years since he'd left MI-6 to work on his own as a freelance agent, he'd come to know most of the regular players. Those who did it for the money. Those who did it for the thrill. Those who wanted to serve but had been disenchanted by bureaucratic bullshit getting in the way of action. Like him.

But that night there were two people the CIA told him to use. One he knew and considered a friend. The other a stranger, but not new to the game, he'd been told. Those two people were responsible for providing intelligence information. The rest of the unit was to engage the compound where it was suspected that a DEA agent was being held. Their mission had been to confirm that the hostage was alive and to extract him if possible.

A task like that relied more on intel than it did on men with guns. That was why two had been chosen to gather and provide the information that the team would need.

Tarak knew one of the two was a traitor.

Unfortunately his first clue that the mission had gone to shit was when he heard shots being fired ahead of schedule. He hadn't given the command to move forward but the explosives were suddenly triggered. A shower of gunfire over their heads had them all running for cover. The guerillas working for the drug lord were behind them in the jungle instead of at their posts inside the compound where they were supposed to be.

Tarak had immediately called for a retreat but their communication had been compromised and all he'd heard was static.

He'd found the bodies of Sheppard, O'Neill and Grace on his way out. All of them his men. It had been Grace, clinging to his last breath, that had cost Tarak the wound to his leg. He'd been lifting him when he got hit from behind. By the time he fell to his knees Grace was already dead.

His only recourse had been to run.

Once more Tarak kneaded the muscles in his leg, harder this time so he could feel the pain and remind himself that he was alive.

Why had fate saved him? Was he a better man? He doubted it.

Sheppard had been a money-hungry bastard but good at his work. O'Neill had been a marvel with explosives, and he had taken an unnatural thrill in blowing things up. But Grace was neither. Grace had been a friend. A loner. A good soldier. He'd had Tarak's back more than once. He'd been trustworthy and in the soldier-for-hire business that kind of reputation was gold.

And now his body was rotting someplace in a South American jungle. Food for the native inhabitants.

Grace didn't deserve that. None of them did. On the way out of that mess what consumed Tarak was why he had survived. He could see no reason why fate had been so kind to him. The dark thoughts had forced him to seek answers, and the only place he could think to begin such a journey was here. Among his mother's people.

He'd been right. After a few weeks at the monastery with help from his mother's uncle, Punab, he'd started to realize it was time to let go of the guilt. Time to move on with this life.

Which ultimately led him to the question…what next? He'd been thinking about his future when the fever had grabbed hold of him. It had occurred to him, even as he felt his fever spiking, that the wound in his leg should have been healing. Only it hadn't been.

The next thing he knew he was waking up in a dark room with a nun wearing a sweat-stained wimple leaning over him.

And there was the other nun. With the strange habit and the skin that seemed to glow.

Tarak shook his head. It had been the fever. It must have been. It had grabbed control of his mind and had shown him ridiculous images. A woman who glowed with gray eyes that did not fit her face.

Had she even been real?

The answer to his question had him gasping. He moved around one of the orchid bunches in his path and froze. His breath caught as he tried to process what he was seeing.

He watched a waif—for surely she was not human—carefully sponge water over her arm, her breasts, her belly and her hips. Letting the droplets crawl down her body into a flat basin under her feet.

Tarak was on the east side of the compound, away from where he knew the monks studied in the morning. He would have expected the courtyard to be empty until noon, but here was the mystery woman from his delirium in the midst of her bath. The partition she used to block the view of onlookers closed her off to the west side of the courtyard, but she obviously hadn't expected anyone to be walking along the east corridor.

There was no question it was her. He knew without seeing the color of her eyes. They were closed. Maybe to better feel the touch of the sponge and water as she ran the rough material over her body. Or maybe simply because she'd gotten soap in her eyes. Whatever the reason, he was grateful because it kept her from being aware of his presence for a time. With the three-sided screen at her back it was as if she was on display just for him.

His personal Venus.

He'd been wrong about the fever stealing his sanity. Her skin did glow. A luminescent sheen that made her almost ethereal. He yearned to touch her. It wasn't just the natural hunger of man for a woman. Although based on his body's quick and urgent response there was that as well. It was like being in the presence of art. Like a marble statue that cried out to be caressed. Only this woman wasn't cold stone, she was living flesh.

She dropped low to dip her sponge in the water, swishing it about. Her eyes opened. He could see her lashes flicker as she concentrated on her calves. Then she reached her hand over her back, the sponge barely making it a quarter of the way down her spine. Suddenly the temptation to help her finish the job was too much.

He stepped forward, forgetting to accommodate his injury by letting his right leg take the bulk of his weight, and a rush of pain shot from his thigh to his brain, forcing a small sound past his lips.

Instantly the waif became aware of his presence. Her arms wrapped around her breasts and the sponge dropped into the pool of water at her feet. Her eyes were round with fear and Tarak felt instantly ashamed. In reality he'd behaved no better than a Peeping Tom. But while he chastised himself for it, he certainly didn't regret it. He wouldn't have missed this show for the world.

Her eyes, however, were still wide with terror.

"I'm not going to hurt you," he said gruffly in English although he repeated the phrase in Hindi.

He assumed her fear stemmed from the thought that he would rape her, but after his words she stood slowly. One arm shielded her femininity from him. The other she wrapped securely around small but pert breasts.

"Do not come any closer," she said in English.

"I won't. I promise," he replied. "You didn't expect anyone to be on this side of the courtyard?"

"They are all in study. I did not expect you to be up and walking so far."

Tarak nodded, then glanced around the washing area. "You bathe here instead of with your sisters down by the river?"

An irrational bolt of anger accompanied his statement. Yes, the monks were celibate but they were still men. There were times a man's sexuality couldn't be so easily controlled with meditation. A woman so beautiful it hurt to look at her could incite the weak-willed to dangerous acts.

"Yes. I cannot bathe in the river."

He heard her words, but they made no sense. "Well, you shouldn't bathe here. Anyone might come along and…"

"Like you."

"Worse than me."

"If you mean the monks, they know better than to touch me. The villagers, too. I am safe from everyone who knows me, but you do not. You must stay back."

"Have I taken a step forward?"

Slowly she shook her head.

There, he thought, satisfied. The beginning of trust. "I'm not a boy to be controlled by my desire. But if I were..." He smiled softly. "You would certainly be a danger to my self-control. Do you have something to dry yourself off?"

He watched her glance toward the robe she'd left hanging on the edge of the partition, but he realized she would have to either drop her arms or turn around and give him an altogether different view of her body to reach it.

A gentlemen would have turned his back. Tarak could almost hear his father's stiff English voice in his head ordering him to turn around and allow the woman her privacy. That nostalgia for his father won out against a hard urge to see if her ass was as shapely as the rest of her.

Tarak turned his back to her. "Hurry," he warned.

He heard the ruffle of movement as she stepped out of the basin and reached for her covering. He counted to what he was sure was a fair five seconds in his head before turning again. The silk material she wore fluttered to her feet and he sighed with disappointment.

"Who are you?" he wanted to know.

An expression crossed over her face that he couldn't

name. Sadness or maybe confusion, as if she didn't know how to answer such a basic question.

"Your name," he said, making it easier for her.

"I am Lilith."

It didn't fit her, not at all. But he didn't press. "Your surname?"

She shook her head. "I have no surname. My…father would not give me his."

He didn't know what to say to that so he offered his own name as a way of building further trust. "I'm Tarak Hammer-Smith. My father was English, but my mother was Indian. She was a niece to Punab. It is how I came to be here."

"I thought you came to be here because of a bullet hole in your leg."

Tarak ignored the implied censure and asked his own question. "Why are you here?"

He didn't think she would answer, but he had to ask it anyway. She was a jewel, he thought. Half woman, half creature. So completely beautiful. But she was tucked away in the jungle among lepers, nuns and celibate monks. It made no sense.

"Are you a Catholic missionary?"

She shook her head. "I am here because I have nowhere else to go. Because I choose to stay."

"You came to my room a few nights ago."

"You were in pain. Sometimes I can help make pain go away."

"You're a healer?"

Again, she shook her head. "No."

"But you brought medicine. I remember drinking from a cup and then…"

And then the pain had stopped. Almost as if he'd gone numb from the roots of his hair to his toes. He hadn't been asleep and whatever he'd sipped had done nothing to reduce his fever. But the next thing he knew the nun was leaning over his leg with a small knife in her hand.

She'd found part of a bullet fragment the medic he'd gone to in Monteria had left behind. The extraction should have been excruciating, but he hadn't felt a thing. Funny that it all came back to him now. But why shouldn't it? He'd been awake the entire time.

"What was in that cup?"

"I need to get back to the village," she said in answer to his question. "First I must dispose of the water. You need to leave."

Dispose of the water? Was it some ritual she needed to perform? "I'll empty the basin for you," Tarak offered as he took a step toward her.

"No. You cannot. I must do it. Stay back. Stay back!"

Tarak stopped in his tracks. He was now only a couple of feet away from her, and he could see the fear return. She was pressed against the partition and couldn't easily get around it. For all intents and purposes he had her trapped.

"Please, you must stay back," she whispered.

"Easy. I told you I'm not going to hurt you. I just want to touch you. I wanted to touch you that night. I remember that. Your skin is so…"

"No," she said and pressed herself against the partition out of reach of his hand. "You cannot. You need to understand. I will hurt you."

"You're not making any sense." But since his ultimate desire was to win her trust, he folded his arms over his chest. "I hate things that don't make sense."

He watched her search for a reply and finally she shrugged her shoulders. "Tough."

He tilted his head back and laughed. It certainly wasn't the answer he'd been expecting. "All right. You win. For now." Tarak took a few steps back from her and with each one he could see her relax. "But, Lilith, I will see you again. And next time you'd better come with some answers."

She said nothing and so he began to head back to his room. Then he stopped as the image of her body came to him, an image he would enjoy conjuring for some time to come. Turning, he saw that she was wrapping the ties around her arms to secure the billowing silk to her body.

"Lilith?"

She snapped her head up, no doubt surprised he was still close. "Yes?"

"It is an interesting necklace. But if you'll pardon me, I must say that I don't think it suits you."

Chapter 4

Lilith stared up at the straw roof of her hut and considered her next move. Considering she was into her second hour of thinking, she feared the answers wouldn't quickly be forthcoming.

It was his fault. The stranger's. No, not stranger, Tarak.

She'd gone up to the monastery to clear her mind so that she could think rationally about what needed to be done. Now all she could think about was his gaze on her, looking at her in a way that she'd never been looked at before.

She'd been desired before, but it had been different then. She'd been barely more than a child. Just thirteen. But her father's brother called her closer to a woman than a girl. A temptation, he'd said. She remembered the look in his eyes whenever he stared at her and thought again of Tarak. Definitely different.

Her uncle hadn't listened to the warnings that she shouldn't be touched. Perhaps he should have known better, but that was her father's fault. Her father had only told others in the village where she lived that she was not to be touched because she was cursed.

Unclean.

It was what she believed, too, until she began to understand that what she could do went beyond super-stition. Beyond her father's hatred.

On that day her uncle caught her alone. He pro-fessed that he didn't believe in curses. He said he would take her to wife if she behaved and did everything he wanted. She remembered the bolt of fear that had shot through her system and how that had caused her skin to dampen with what she believed back then was merely sweat.

She tried to run, but he caught her. Then he tore away the heavy coverings that she wore in layers to protect herself from the cold as well as from incidental contact, and she watched as his hand roughly cupped her barely there breast.

Suddenly his eyes popped open and he hissed through his teeth, struggling to catch his breath. Before she could pull away from him he fell on her. Dead weight.

Her father found her struggling to crawl out from underneath the body. He blamed her for enticing his brother, for causing his death. For being born cursed.

She tried to explain she hadn't meant to kill him. She just had.

That night he took her to a monastery in Nepal where it was known that one of the monks would soon be leaving for India. He'd warned the monk of her perfidy and insisted that she live among the outcast. The monk obeyed and brought her to this village.

What revenge she might have if her father knew how she'd flourished here. In this place she wasn't seen as inherently evil or cursed. Here she helped people and worked to find spiritual fulfillment that would help her to someday forgive herself for taking a life.

Yes, he would be outraged to know that she had made a home here.

Lilith bolted up from her sleeping mat as a question occurred to her. Her father hated her. She'd always known that. As a child she imagined it was because of her sickness. As an adult she came to believe it was because she'd caused him sadness, the death of a wife he must have loved greatly.

But the woman who'd given birth to her wasn't his wife. According to Jackie, Petra had been chosen from a family in Tibet who were well paid for their youngest daughter. Her father, Gensen, was from a village far south of that. Had he even known Lilith's surrogate mother before her birth?

Lilith struggled to recall what she'd read earlier. There had been so much and it had all been so distressing that it was hard to remember the specifics. She reached for the necklace around her throat and looked to the laptop that still sat on her desk.

"Only the information about me," she promised herself as she got up and walked over to the computer.

She removed the flash drive from the necklace and booted up the computer. Then she walked through the steps Sister Peter had given her earlier to access and read the information in the files. She searched for and found what she was looking for.

Gensen.

She clicked on the folder and selected the first file in it.

Gensen was a proud man. It was his pride that drew me to him in the first place… And made me want to crush it…

Lilith continued to read about how Jackie had met the Buddhist monk. Once a leader among his people, he had been on the path to enlightenment. But Gensen had not been prepared for Jackie's unique brand of temptation. She didn't immediately offer him her body. Instead she played on his intelligence, his spirituality and his pride. She made him believe that the two of them were connected in some universal way.

Then she seduced him. Once his vows of celibacy were behind him and he considered himself fallen from the path, he no longer fought her control over him. She asked for and was given his life essence. Once she had what she needed, she left him broken and humbled.

Lilith leaned back in her chair as a wave of regret and sadness threatened to smother her.

"You did not hate me because of what I was or

what I did. You hated me because of her. Because I was part of her."

She knew from the stories that her father had told her that Petra had gone into premature labor with her and that before the doctor had pulled Lilith free from the woman, she had died. Then the doctor who first held Lilith died, too. A quick-thinking nurse with a heavy blanket had pulled the child from the dying man's hands and managed to save her. Because Lilith had been responsible for Petra's death, Gensen told Lilith that her mother's family had disowned her and that all she had left was him.

Doctor. Nurse. The story had always seemed odd to Lilith. All the babies born in the village where she'd grown up and even here in this village were born at home with only a midwife in attendance.

Not her.

Jackie must have been there. She must have waited to see what her egg had produced. Then she had handed her over to Gensen to raise…why? Maybe as a means of protection. Or possibly Jackie wanted to put Lilith someplace where she could easily find her again.

How angry Jackie must have been when she returned to Gensen's village only to find that he'd banished Lilith to India. Considering what she'd read about Jackie, Lilith had to wonder whether or not her father was still alive. It seemed likely that the woman called Arachne would have dispatched him when his usefulness was over.

Lilith didn't know how she felt about that. Surely she

should be sad if her father was murdered. She had always carried the sadness of killing the woman she'd believed to be her mother. But Petra had been an innocent. Her father was not.

For that matter neither was Jackie. Lilith felt no remorse over her passing.

Vaguely she wondered how many monasteries Jackie had searched before finally finding the one near a leper colony where her daughter lived. Her visits had started years ago. If Lilith had been looking for it back then she might have sensed a certain satisfaction in Jackie's expression when they first met. But of course, Lilith hadn't been looking for it. Naively she'd accepted the story the woman spun never realizing that she was in the presence of her mother.

Or the presence of evil.

The memory of each visit would need to be scrutinized. Every word exchanged, analyzed for new meaning. But before any of that happened, Lilith had to make a decision about the information that was now in her control. She was about to turn off the offensive machine when a file name caught her eye.

Children.

Children. Not child. Unable to help herself, Lilith clicked on the file and began to read about Jackie's other…offspring.

Two other women. Both with unique abilities. Both her half sisters.

Eventually Lilith turned off the laptop. It was too

much to learn in one day. About her mother, her father and her sisters. Sisters. Related to her.

Family.

The crush of emotions made her nauseous.

Three women all spawned in a lab from the eggs of a woman who was clearly immoral. What Lilith was given was only a third of the entire picture. Jackie said the pieces needed to be put together, but Lilith wasn't sure what her mother's intention had been. Whether she imagined her three children joining together for some nefarious purpose or if somehow the three flash drives were connected.

It didn't matter. Lilith's piece would never be joined to complete any puzzle that Jackie had a role in creating.

And what about her sisters? Did they want to claim their full inheritance? If, like Lilith, Jackie had given the two babies to other people to raise, they might not share Jackie's depravity. They might be just as horrified by the information as Lilith. What if at this moment they were seeking her out, hoping that Lilith might have some answers for them?

She needed to find a way to contact them. Instantly she thought of Sister Peter. She would know how to find someone. She was forever talking about how the Internet was such a powerful tool. Bringing the entire world together. Once Lilith found her sisters Sister Peter would know which authorities could be trusted. As an American, she had a deep understanding of justice and the system that upheld it.

But to use her like that, Lilith would have to tell the nun why she needed her help. The burden of Jackie's files was too much to share. Lilith couldn't claim to be an expert on the world, but she was at least savvy enough to know that the information in her possession could make her a target. Certainly the people listed on these files would want to find this information once they learned of Jackie's death. Find it and destroy it along with anyone who might continue to blackmail them.

Her mind wandered back to the man in the monastery. The brothers called him a warrior. Warriors fought. But who did he fight for? A man of violence, did he use his skills to help or to hurt people?

Dismissing the idea before she let her mind formulate it fully, she knew she would not ask Tarak for help. It was too risky. She couldn't involve anyone she didn't trust. Better to keep the information hidden rather than risk exposure.

Which meant she was on her own in trying to find a way to locate these other women. She would see if they had received a spider from their mother. Then together they could decide what to do next. The simplest solution would be to destroy it all. Lilith, however, would wait until she had their counsel.

Outside she heard a noise. Acting quickly, she hid the computer under her sleeping mat. She returned the memory stick to its hiding place in the necklace and dropped the spider inside her silk coverall.

Another helicopter. This one circled overhead searching for a place to land. The pilot must have spotted the small landing area, because it began its descent.

"My, we're becoming popular around here," Sister Joseph said as she hustled her round body over to where Lilith stood in the center of the village. "Do you know what this is about?"

"No, Sister." It wasn't a lie but she knew it could not be a coincidence.

Calmly Sister Joseph folded her arms over her large bosom. "Are we in trouble, Lilith? I'm not asking because I am upset. I just want to know what we're dealing with. I have more than my sisters to think about. I feel responsibility toward the villagers, as well."

Lilith turned to find Sister Peter rushing up to join them. She stopped short and also crossed her arms over her breasts. She looked as concerned as Sister Joseph.

"I do not know what this is about. But I cannot promise it will not lead to trouble," she said honestly to both of them. "Be alert."

Sister Peter nodded. "I'll round up the villagers. Let them know to keep the children close."

Lilith waited as once more it was the children leading the parade for the visitors coming out of the jungle. Until their parents intervened and pulled them away from the excitement. At first the children resisted, but ultimately they obeyed, leaving only the helicopter's passengers.

Lilith counted five large men of varying colors and race, all outwardly armed. Some with more than one weapon attached to different body parts. They looked as fierce as she imagined they wanted to. More men of violence.

But it was the woman in front of them that caught her attention.

About Lilith's height, the woman's skin was a lighter shade of brown than Lilith's, but her eyes…they were Jackie's eyes. Not the color, but the shape. There was no doubt she was looking at another one of Jackie's daughters.

"Let me guess," the woman said to Lilith, opening her arms in welcome. "You are Lilith."

"Yes," she whispered even as she felt the air clog in her throat.

The woman smiled broadly and widened her arms even more. "Well, hell. Come give your big sister Echo a hug!"

Chapter 5

The woman stopped a few feet short of Lilith. Her arms dropped to her sides. "Oh, that's right. No hugging, is there? Oh well, we'll just air kiss and call it a reunion."

The words made sense, but Lilith couldn't decipher her tone. Nor did she understand the woman's attitude. They were two women who were linked by a biological bond. They were relatives coming together for the first time. Yet Lilith could find no sign of the significance of this moment in the woman's voice. She seemed cavalier about their meeting. Not relieved. Not happy. Not afraid.

Nothing.

"You found me," Lilith realized. "How?"

"Mummy's little gift to me," Echo told her. "I have to assume you got one, too. A special gift, that is?"

"I…" Lilith's throat locked up. "I do not think we should talk about this in front of others."

"Oooooh. A cautious little thing, aren't you? That's good. That means you're smarter than I was probably going to give you credit for being."

Sister Peter stepped up to stand beside Lilith. She was touched by the sign of support from the sister, but still Lilith would rather Sister Peter not say anything. "Lilith, what is this woman saying? Is she your sister?"

"The name is Echo." Echo stretched out her hand to the nun but quickly pulled it back. "Oh, sorry. I keep doing that. This is a leper colony, right? Maybe I would do better not touching anything while I'm here. So, a nun? Wicked. Are you my sister's friend?"

"I am," Sister Peter said.

"Then you must know about her loss. Our mother— a mother we didn't even know we had—is gone. Killed. I've come to grieve with the only family I have left. I'm sure you can appreciate that."

"Killed?" Lilith repeated, focusing on only that. Killed was very different from dead.

"Yes," Echo relayed. "It was awful. When I heard I was angry. So hurt. But it's true. I had my people verify the information. Mummy was murdered by a woman named Allison Gracelyn. You don't know her, but our two families have been at odds for years. Where Mummy succeeded in making something important of herself, Allison's mother failed. Allison never got over that. She wanted revenge. More than that, she wanted to steal our mother's empire. Something you must understand by now is quite…extensive."

Lilith said nothing, but she felt Echo's eyes boring into her, studying her as if to learn something that Lilith didn't want to reveal. She tried to focus on the story that Echo was telling her, but all she could think was…*danger*.

"Or do you?" Echo wondered aloud. "In this backwater village maybe you don't even know what…" She stopped herself and shook her head. "It doesn't matter. All that matters is that I'm here. You and I are connected. Isn't that amazing?"

It should have been, but amazement was the last thing Lilith felt.

"We must do something to celebrate," Echo continued. "A feast and some wine. We can sit and talk. I want to know you, sister. Intimately. Just like I'm sure you want to know everything there is to know about me."

"Lilith, I must go and see to my duties," Sister Peter interrupted. "You're welcome to use the meeting hall to talk and get…acquainted. Also, I'm sure the monks would welcome your guests."

"Absolutely." Sister Joseph beamed. "Please make yourself welcome. Any friend of Lilith's is naturally welcome here. We'll leave you to catch up. I am sorry for your loss. Both of you. Sometimes even those people who don't play a large role in our life can still make a horrible dent when they leave it. God bless you both."

Echo clutched a hand to her heart. "God bless you, too, Sister. Thank you for those kind and meaningful words."

Lilith watched Echo watch the nun walk away. She watched her make a gesture behind her back and thought again that every word she said would have to be scrutinized for truth.

"Nuns, huh?" Echo asked. "This place is crawling with them. Does that mean you're one, too? Makes sense, I suppose, since you can't ever let anyone touch you."

"No. I'm not a nun," Lilith said carefully. Instinctively she knew that information was power to her sister and the less said the less power she might have.

"We could leave here," Echo offered Lilith. "I could snatch you up in my helicopter. We could find the closest piece of civilization and hope they have decent curry. Wouldn't that be fun?"

Lilith shook her head. She wasn't going anywhere with this woman if she could help it. "I prefer not to leave the village. The meeting area is this way. There we can sit and talk. We have food, but no wine."

"Oh, well. Boys."

Lilith started walking in the direction of the lodge that was referred to as the meeting hall. It was where the sisters took their meals together. Prayed together. Where the elders in the village met to discuss issues. It was a simple single-room structure, but it would serve their needs. Glancing back over her shoulder, she could see Echo's men following close behind, their faces strangely neutral as they passed many inhabitants who were covered to hide their faces or missing limbs.

She'd labeled them as men of violence and instantly

the label made her think of Tarak. But these men seemed different to her. Colder. Tarak's face had never been so neutral. Certainly not when he was in the grip of the fever. And definitely not when he was looking at her.

They reached the wood structure and Lilith led them inside. Sunab, daughter of one of the village elders, offered to feed the guests so that Lilith could visit with the newcomers. Lilith accepted the offer and together they sat at a long table. Echo on one side, Lilith on the other, Her men sat at the opposite end apart from the two women. None of them spoke.

"So," Echo began. "What shall we dish about?"

"I am sorry…dish? I speak English. Sister Peter has taught me some idioms, but I am not familiar…"

"Dish. Chat. Talk. Converse. I think we should start with Mummy's gift. You got one, too. You don't seem all that surprised by my being here, which means you must have accessed it somehow. Where is it?"

Lilith smiled graciously at Sunab as the girl poured her a cup of water. She reached for it and took a few sips, watching Echo scrunch up her nose at the fruit and flat bread being offered.

"There is another one like us," Lilith said, avoiding the question. "Are you aware of that? Do you know her?"

Echo focused her gaze back on Lilith. "Of course I know we had another sister. She was murdered. Sad that we didn't get to know her. But she was also killed by that woman I mentioned. Not her directly. One of her minions. Still, Gracelyn was behind it."

"You make this woman sound dangerous."

Echo chuckled. "Allison Gracelyn is a very powerful, very bad woman. Her mother founded an academy where Allison now sits on the board. A school for girls. She trains them in her image. These pupils destroyed our mother, acting on Gracelyn's orders. Then they went after our sister. Dangerous? Yes, I would say she's dangerous. But that doesn't mean I'm afraid of her."

"Of course not," Lilith said. "Our sister. Who was she?"

"Her name was Kwan-Sook. She was special like us. A real giant of a woman, if you know what I mean. But deformed. As an invalid she was easy for Gracelyn's girls to eliminate."

Killed, murdered, eliminated. The words came so easily. "This woman killed Jackie. Then Kwan-Sook. Why?"

"I told you why. For revenge. For the information in Mummy's control. Information is power. Information over powerful people is, well…really valuable stuff. Anyone would kill for that."

Not anyone. But at least Echo confirmed Lilith's belief that information was a tool that she liked to use. "I meant to say why now? Was there something that happened that triggered this woman to act?"

Echo lifted her shoulders. "Who knows. Maybe she stumbled upon something. Some thread that led her to Mummy. That doesn't matter. What matters is that there is only us left. And if you think she won't be coming after us and Mummy's gift then you're wrong."

"You think she could find me here?"

"She found Mummy. She can find anyone. So where are you keeping it?"

To ask *Keeping what?* would have been foolish. Lilith didn't completely understand this woman yet. Maybe hopelessly, she still found herself looking for some commonality between them. But she knew one thing for certain. Her sister was no fool.

Keen intelligence resonated in the glint of her brown eyes. Just like they had in Jackie's.

"It is hidden," she answered finally.

Slowly Echo nodded.

"Excellent idea. Precautions are necessary. Have you read everything?"

"No. I could only open some of the files. Others were filled with gibberish.

"Encrypted."

Lilith accepted Echo's statement. "What I did read did not make much sense to me."

It wasn't exactly a lie. For a woman who tried to adhere to Buddhist precepts the acts of depravity those people committed didn't compute. However, Lilith knew that she was deliberately misleading Echo. It was obvious that Echo couldn't hide her disdain for the humble place where she'd found her sister. It might be useful to let her believe that Lilith was as simple and uneducated as Echo wanted to believe she was.

"It is a lot to take in for me, as well. I, too, only had

access to part of the data. But tell me more about you. This skin condition you have. Is it terribly annoying?"

Given the way she reacted when they first met, Lilith had already determined that Echo knew about her condition. Suddenly she felt at a disadvantage. She hadn't read enough to know what skill Echo or the other sister who had been murdered possessed.

"It is manageable. Sometimes I can use it to help people."

The woman's lips turned up in what should have been a smile. "Help people. That's sweet. You're a softy, aren't you? I can tell. Help people. That's priceless."

Echo looked away as if she were studying the structure. Analyzing. Calculating. Lilith could practically hear her brain working.

When she focused her gaze on Lilith once more the smile was gone. "We could do that together. We could take this information and use it somehow to help people."

"How?"

Echo shifted on her bench. "I don't know exactly how this minute. But we'll think about it. We'll discuss it. You'll show me where you've hidden her…computer?"

"Laptop."

"Laptop," Echo repeated slowly. "We'll pool the information that we have and we'll see how we can use it to make this world a better place. Wouldn't that be fun? Two sisters working together to fight evil and injustice. Our first mission would be to take down Allison

Gracelyn and her academy. Finding justice at last for our poor dead mother and sister."

Lilith wondered if Echo could hear the insincerity in her voice. "I think it is important that the right thing be done with the information we have been given."

"Ditto."

No longer able to stay in Echo's company, Lilith stood and worked to keep her knees from trembling. "I have chores I must see to. Please stay and eat."

"Maybe you could get the laptop now. Why wait?"

"I would have to retrieve it from the hiding place. Tomorrow morning would be best as dawn approaches. The forest is not safe after dark. You can sleep here— we have extra mats. Or at the monastery."

"Here is fine," Echo said between clenched teeth. "After all, we still have so much catching up to do. You go do your chores. Then later you can tell me about your life. I will tell you about mine. We can make up stories about our dear Mummy. What it would have been like if she had raised us together. So sad for us. If only we'd had the chance to meet her and know her, everything might have been different."

"I did know her."

Echo blinked. Once. Twice. "Excuse me? What did you say?"

"I said I knew her," Lilith repeated carefully, watching the change ripple over Echo's expression. The facade Echo had presented faltered under true emotion and for the first time Lilith actually believed the emotion that Echo was now displaying: rage.

"Knew her."

"She visited the village. Regularly. She did not tell me who she was. I thought she was a philanthropist. Our benefactress. She gave us much-needed money for medical supplies."

"You spoke to her." Echo's voice was soft and throaty.

"For hours. About the work that needed to be done. About the sacrifice the nuns had made. About religion in general. She was very intelligent and had strong opinions."

"She never mentioned a…daughter?"

"No. No family. Ever. You can imagine how shocking it was to learn that this woman whom I had spoken to so many times was in fact my true mother."

"Yes."

Lilith walked backward toward the door, her eyes on Echo as she watched the woman process what she'd learned. It was like watching a chemical reaction at the point right before the explosion.

"Echo, you should know. You have her eyes. The shape of them. If that is any comfort to you."

Lilith stepped out of the hall, letting the tarp fall back into place. The sound of a fist hitting the table, rattling the cups and serving trays, was loud.

"Ahhhh!" Echo pulled at her short hair until the pain in her skull was almost as much as the pain that seemed to rip through her body. "How could she! Here? To this shitty little mud village! That bitch!"

One of her men made the mistake of shifting in his seat, turning toward Echo as if to offer comfort. Echo stood abruptly, tipping over the bench behind her. She marched to him and slapped him as hard as she could across the face.

"What are you looking at?"

The pain in her hand and the pain she'd inflicted did nothing to ease the emotional storm that was rolling inside her.

Jackie had visited Lilith. Seen Lilith. Spoken to Lilith. It wasn't fair.

From the moment Echo had read the files on her mother, she'd known an instant connection. All her life she'd grown up knowing she was different. Accepting that she was special. Waiting for a time when she would finally find her place in this world.

She'd found it in the file on her mother. A woman of strength, focus and purpose. But beyond that was ambition. Lots of ambition that had transformed into a ruthless need-to-be-on-top obsession. This is who her mother was.

This is who Echo was.

It was difficult enough learning that there were two other daughters. Harder still to know that her mother had given them each a piece of what rightly should belong to Echo. It was only when she learned that all three drives needed to be brought together to reveal the true scope of her mother's empire that it made sense.

Her mother's inheritance would go to the most worthy.

Who was surely Echo.

She had to be. Because her heart beat the same as Jackie's. Her mind worked the same as Jackie's. Was it wrong to want some acknowledgment that she, more than anyone, was her mother's true heir?

Instead Jackie had come here to Lilith.

What was it about that simple little waif that made her so special? With her pathetic robes and missions of mercy, she was the antithesis of what Echo imagined her mother to be.

Help people?

According to the file, Jackie had never helped another human being in her twisted life. It was part of what Echo loved about her.

No, Lilith wasn't special. Echo wouldn't let her be. Lilith was nothing more than a pathetic afterthought. A genetic mistake who had chosen to hide herself in this wretched village rather than use what she'd been given to make herself stronger. More powerful.

Weak. Not in body like Kwan-Sook. But in mind and will. To Echo that was a greater sin.

"What's next?" This was from her man Kent. Insolent animal, but a ruthless killer. She wanted to hit him, too, but she forced herself to focus.

"We wait until dark. We trash the village and find the laptop."

"She said she hid it," Kent reminded her.

"She lied. No need to hide it from the nuns or the lepers and she had no idea I was coming. Rolf, go watch her. Make sure she doesn't try to take off into the jungle. As soon as it's dark meet back here with your weapons fully loaded."

Rolf jumped up and left. The rest of the men remained, picking at the bread and fruit. Passing time, Echo knew, until they were called upon to kill.

"Sweet little Lilith," Echo murmured. "Mummy may have liked you best, but I can promise you I will have the last word."

Lilith reached her hut and placed a hand over her heart to settle it. How foolish she'd been to think that the women who shared her genes would share her beliefs, as well. Or maybe she was the outsider. Given what she knew about Jackie, maybe Echo and Kwan-Sook had followed in their mother's footsteps of crime and blackmail, while Lilith had been spared. Echo's words about helping people rang so false it was almost comical. All she wanted was the flash drive. And the power that came with it.

Everything else was a lie.

Except her anger over Jackie's visits. If Lilith had any darkness in her soul she might have taken satisfaction in finding the one weapon she had over Echo: jealousy. Sibling rivalry at its worst. There was no mistaking it. Echo was jealous of Lilith's past with their mother. It seemed ridiculous given Echo's cold nature, but if Lilith had to use it she would.

After a deep, meditative breath, Lilith worked through her options. She was certain of two things: Echo couldn't be trusted and Echo couldn't get her hands on Lilith's files. She didn't know if Echo had Kwan-Sook's drive, but it wasn't a chance Lilith was going to take.

She could run now. Hide in the forest. Echo would come looking for her. With her men they were six to Lilith's one. Plus a helicopter to aid in the search.

Subterfuge was more practical. It would buy her the time she needed to find help. Tomorrow she would hand over the laptop; pretend it contained the documents and pray Echo left before she realized the truth.

Once Echo discovered her mistake, she would be back. There was no question. But when she returned Lilith knew that she would have found someone to trust with the information. She knew that because there was no choice.

Calmer now that she understood what needed to be done, she pulled the computer out from under her mat and turned the power on. Patiently, as the sun went down outside, she watched the battery monitor on the screen drop from medium, to low, to empty.

A warning appeared that the computer needed to be powered off. Lilith, however, left it on until the screen went black. She confirmed it would not turn on again and slipped it back under the mat.

Lying wasn't something she practiced much so tomorrow would be a test for her. But it was a test she knew she could not fail.

Echo would not add to the information she'd already received from Jackie. Once Lilith was able to prevent that from happening then she would need to work out how to destroy what Echo had already been given by their mother.

Because there was no doubt in Lilith's mind that her sister was very, very sick.

Chapter 6

When Lilith would look back on this night she would remember the first thing she heard wasn't the gunfire.

It was the shouting.

She sprang up on her mat and knew by her heart rate that her body had reacted faster to the threat than her mind.

Night had fallen, but she hadn't been able to sleep. Hadn't expected to. Instead she'd been rehearsing over and over again the story that she would tell Echo in the morning. A story the woman had to believe.

Only, morning was several hours off and something was already starting. The sudden popping sound left no clue as to the cause of the chaos. Lilith rolled off her mat and reached for the robe, then stopped. She could feel the dew on her skin, could see it glow even in the darkness.

Tonight her curse could be her salvation.

Dressed only in her short slip and the necklace she hadn't removed, she found the leather satchel that held the laptop and slung it over her shoulder. She was prepared to face Echo and her men, but when she pulled the heavy tarp back from her hut it was as if the world had suddenly erupted into flames.

People were running with children in their arms. She could see the nuns out of habit running alongside them, directing them away from the center of the village where flames were consuming individual homes as well as the meeting lodge.

Why? Why had she needed to do this?

"Oh, Lilith! Come out, come out wherever you are!"

Lilith turned her head at the sound of Echo's voice. Her shouting could be heard even over the cries of the children. Without hesitating, Lilith followed the call until she was standing in the center of the village amidst a whirl of smoke and falling ash. Through the haze she could make out Echo's men holding torches in their hands. Deliberately setting them to the straw and mud-caked roofs until bursts of flames ignited. Some of the villagers tried to yell at them, some tried to fight, but any resistance was met with gunfire. Shots that were quick and lethal.

"Stop." Lilith knew her voice wouldn't carry. The word was barely a whisper. But what she was seeing, what these men were doing… She had never known that such things could exist.

With so many of the shelters on fire, the village glowed orange. Lilith searched for the woman who had orchestrated the attack. She started to run farther into the smoke but stopped when she saw Echo standing a few feet away, her booted foot on top of Sister Peter's head, grinding it into the dirt.

Lilith jolted forward. "Let her go!"

Echo glanced up and smiled. She had changed her clothes. When she arrived she'd been in khaki cargo pants and a T-shirt. Now she wore all black along with a vest that was practical rather than fashionable. Like her men, she had a gun holster under each arm. One of the guns dangled casually in her hand like an extension of her body.

"Sister! How smart of you to come so quickly. Like I said, I knew you were no dummy. You know what I want."

"I was going to give it to you in the morning. You did not have to do this."

"You were going to give it to me." She laughed. "You know, I actually believe you. That proves how pathetic you are. You don't surrender information like this. You hold on to it. You fight for it. You kill for it. Because there has never been anything so valuable."

"Value is subjective."

"That's right, my little Buddhist philosopher."

Lilith watched as Echo motioned to one of her men standing only a few feet away. "She's got it on her. The satchel. Go get it," she ordered.

Lilith didn't move. Instead she held on to the strap

of the bag and struggled to take her eyes off Sister Peter, who had managed to pull her face out of the dirt. The nun's eyes were wide with fear, but Lilith could see anger, too. And a silent plea not to give in to the threat.

"Let Sister Peter go. She has nothing to do with this. I will give you the computer."

Echo tilted her head, a nasty scowl forming on her face. "Don't tell me what to do. Just because you were Mummy's favorite, don't think that makes you special."

"I only want you to go."

"Then hand over the bag."

"Once you let her go."

"Uric, take the damn satchel," Echo commanded.

Echo's man moved with determination to where Lilith stood. He pulled back a beefy hand and back-handed her across the face, wanting to knock her down first before removing the bag from her shoulder. Lilith barely had time to feel the sting of the blow before he was on the ground at her feet, convulsing. A few seconds later the convulsions stopped.

"Oooohh. That's sick. He barely touched you and he's dead. You're a real menace, aren't you?"

Echo bent down and pulled the nun up by the roots of her hair until she was on her knees. Sister Peter tried to struggle, but Echo's superior strength was evident. Lilith could do nothing but watch as Echo pushed the point of the gun against her friend's temple.

"Drop the bag and take a few steps back or I will kill her."

Lilith complied immediately. She removed the strap from around her body, dropped the bag onto the ground and took several steps away from it. She would have given Echo anything to spare Sister Peter's life.

"There. Take it and go."

But Echo wasn't moving and the gun remained at Sister Peter's head. "Rolf, go get the bag."

"But she touched it," he said, hesitating.

"Good point." Echo lifted her gun toward Lilith.

"The poison doesn't transfer," Lilith said quickly. There was no reason to lie when she wanted Echo to take the bag and leave. "It binds with water. And it can pass through material, but once it leaves my skin it's harmless."

"Hear that, Rolf? You're as safe as a kitten. Go get me the bag."

Done with their tasks of destruction, Echo's remaining men rejoined her in the center of the village. The large man with the light skin moved to obey her order. He brought the bag to Echo and pulled out the laptop. Lilith watched as he tried to power it up.

He shook his head.

"The battery died," Lilith interjected. "I had it on for a few hours but then it died. You can see we have no electricity here."

Echo tugged on Sister Peter's hair hard until she cried out. "Do you think I'm an idiot?"

"No."

"Mummy sent you the laptop so you could read the

files, but she sent the files separately. Do you know how I know this? Because that's exactly what she did for me. Where's the spider?"

Lilith hesitated.

"You say you don't care about the information for yourself. So that can't be the reason you're not handing it over. Which must mean you just don't want me to have it."

"I do not."

Echo's jaw dropped in apparent shock. "Such disloyalty from my own damn family. You have five seconds to give me what I want or I shoot the nun. One. Two. Three…"

"Wait!" Lilith reached under the cotton slip she wore and pulled the spider out from between her breasts. "This is it. This is what you want."

Echo practically glowed with triumph. "Yes. That is what I want. Gaudy, isn't it? I couldn't be bothered to actually wear mine. Silly me for thinking that I was the only one who got the necklace. That it was special. Now I don't feel so bad for tossing it. After all, it's only what's inside that's important."

"Let her go. I will give you the necklace."

"Again with the orders. I can shoot her, shoot you and take the damn thing for myself."

"You could," Lilith agreed. "But it might be a while before the poison in my system is neutralized and you can take the chance of removing the necklace. Unless you brought protective gear with you, that is. I said it doesn't transfer, but it can be absorbed. Some materials can delay it. Most do not."

"Clever, sister," Echo conceded. "Fine. Straight up. You toss me the necklace and I let your friend go."

Lilith reached for the chain around her neck and tugged hard. She looked down at the ugly gold spider in her hand then at Echo.

"Don't." Sister Peter was still fighting Echo's hold on her, shaking her head from side to side.

Lilith could see the stubborn gleam in her eyes, but her stubbornness was useless against Echo. It was a choice. Between the harm that Echo might do versus the harm that Echo would do if Lilith didn't give her what she wanted.

She couldn't take the chance.

Lilith tossed the necklace and watched as it fell at Echo's feet.

Dropping to her haunches, while still keeping a grip on the sister, Echo plucked up the spider and smiled at the fearsome design.

"Yes, same as mine. My word, did Mummy have bad taste in jewelry."

Then before Lilith had a chance to blink, the gun in Echo's hand fired. Sister Peter fell lifelessly to the ground as the blood rushed out of her skull and into the dirt.

Echo stood, turning her gun on Lilith. "You didn't actually think I was going to let her live, did you?"

Lilith had no air in her lungs to answer.

"Oh. I think you did."

She could feel the heat of the fires burning around

her. She could smell the smoke and see the villagers racing to carry pots of water from the river, but her brain wasn't working any longer. It wasn't telling her to run or hide. It wasn't telling her to fight.

All she could think was that they had made a deal. The necklace for Sister Peter.

Echo hadn't kept her part.

Stepping over the body, Echo moved closer. If she moved another few feet, Lilith might be able to reach out and touch her. She remained frozen.

Another footstep. One more. But Echo stopped just short of where Lilith wanted her.

The gun was aimed at her head. Death, a topic she had studied so closely as part of her faith, a topic she knew so well because of who she was, was only a trigger pull away. Lilith wasn't frightened. Her only concern was how fast and in what form she would be reborn so that she could fight Echo in her next life.

"We have what we need. Kill her and let's go," said one of her men, who appeared bored by the night's proceedings.

Echo whipped her head around. "Don't distract me!"

In that second Lilith acted, but when she reached forward with her hands to touch her sister's face she was stopped by a wall that she could not see.

"Uh, uh, uh," Echo chastised. "I have my special gifts, too."

Lilith pushed again but whatever it was, it was strong enough to keep her from touching Echo.

"It seems you're not quite the good little girl you pretend to be. You didn't hesitate to try to kill me. Me, your only remaining sister. Mummy actually might have been proud. At least you're not quite as pathetic as I thought. You know, I don't think I will kill you. Better to know you're here, rotting in this forsaken jungle. Cursing me with every breath and knowing that you couldn't do anything to stop me."

Another gunshot fired, this one from a distance. Lilith was sure that it was heading in her direction. Echo's henchmen doing what Echo had chosen not to? But instead she could see the bullet bounce off Echo's invisible shield. It might have hit her head, but instead fell harmlessly into the dirt. Echo turned toward the gunshot in reaction and in that second Lilith could feel her hand press closer through whatever it was that Echo was using to block her out.

One more centimeter.

But Echo quickly returned her attention to her biggest threat.

"It seems one of these villagers found a gun. I wasn't expecting that. I suppose it is time to leave. Anyone makes another move and I swear I *will* destroy this village and every living thing in it." This Echo shouted to everyone within hearing distance. "Goodbye, sister. Say…thank you for not killing me."

Lilith didn't answer. Echo merely shrugged. "Fine. Be like that. Just be grateful I'm a woman of my word."

She started to walk away then turned back. "Oh wait. That's right. I'm not a woman of my word."

Echo spun around quickly, anxious to see the expression of stunned disbelief when the bullet found her sister's stomach. Instead of flesh her bullet met only air as Lilith darted off for the jungle.

"I can't believe she ran. It's like she didn't trust me."

"Should we track her down?" Rolf asked.

Echo considered her options. She had what she needed. Lilith was nothing like Kwan-Sook. She had no criminal empire at her disposal, no access to any contacts that might be dangerous to her or her plans.

There was nothing Lilith could do that would amount to any sort of threat. And what Echo had told her sister was true. There was pleasure in knowing Lilith was stuck in this lost part of the world, helpless. Really, Echo had just wanted to kill Lilith for the fun of it. Chasing her into the jungle to kill her for pleasure was self-indulgent.

There was a world out there for Echo to conquer, after all.

"Not necessary. She's of no concern to me any longer." Echo dropped the spider that was still in her hand, the last legacy from her mother, into her front vest pocket. "Go fire up the chopper. We're leaving."

Tarak slunk back into the jungle away from the black helicopter. He still didn't understand how he had missed his shot, but now wasn't the time to ask questions.

Slowly he moved into the trees and bushes as if he were being sucked back into a black hole. A noise behind him caught his ear.

Breathing. Running.

Instantly he turned, prepared to fire another shot.

He crouched low among the heavy foliage and waited for what he believed to be his enemy to emerge from a thicket northeast of his position. But when the figure burst through the trees into the small clearing he instantly recognized the form.

He stood and moved to catch her around the waist, preventing her from going any farther, but she quickly spotted him when he stood and stopped in her tracks. Not wanting her to make any noise, he thought the easiest course of action would be to secure her in his grasp with a hand over her mouth, but before he could move she was back-stepping out of his reach.

Gasps of high-pitched air escaped her mouth, but that was the only noise she made. He moved to put his finger to his lips but he didn't know if she could see his action in the dark. Or, for that matter, recognize who he was.

But she wasn't calling out for help. Or screeching in a way that might have invited visitors.

Good girl.

Holstering his gun, he used his hands to motion that she should crouch low. He put them over his head once to indicate his intentions and then again made the crouching motion. Following his own advice, he moved out of the small opening, closer to a thicket of trees that would secure his cover.

He waited for a whisper from her, or some other sound to announce her confusion. But there was none. Only a small rustling motion as she, too, buried herself amongst the trees only a few paces away.

The group emerging from the burning village felt no need to hide their presence. The men moved in advance of the woman whom Tarak had seen at the center of the chaos. Short cropped hair, purposeful stride, but with a figure that screamed all woman. He hadn't seen her features, but he recognized her as the woman who shot the nun.

She barked some orders to hurry everyone along as they climbed inside the chopper. In the next instant the blades started to whirl until they were fast enough to lift the machine off the ground. An abrupt movement to his right let him know that his friend wasn't prepared to let them go that easily.

He reached out with his hand to grab hold of something that would stop her chase, but she averted his grasp and sprinted forward. He might have been concerned if he wasn't certain that by the time she got to the clearing the chopper would be gone.

Relaxed, he stood and followed the path she had taken. She stood in the indentation of mud where the front wheel had been and looked defeated as her eyes followed the line and sound of the machine as it lifted into the night sky.

"They won't go far," he informed her. He pulled a knife from his belt and held it up for her to see the outline of it in his hand. "Fuel line. They've got a few miles, I would guess. They'll either recognize their situation and land or they'll crash. Either way they'll be far enough away from here not to do any more harm."

Tarak took a step closer. Lilith took a step back. It was like a dance but only she seemed to know the steps.

"You have to help me."

That had him smiling. "I believe I just did."

"No, we have to go after them. Whether they land or crash we have to find her. We have to get it back."

It. The necklace he'd seen exchanged. He remembered it from when he'd seen it dangling from Lilith's neck between breasts that had been far more interesting to him. He didn't like the necklace then. He certainly didn't like it any better now.

"Retrieving the necklace won't bring the nun back to life."

"You saw it happen?"

He had. Bursts of orange light from the village had gotten his attention during his nightly walk to stretch and strengthen his leg. By the time the shots were fired he was already on his way down the hill from the monastery, taking his time to move in the shadows and assess the situation before he jumped in. By the time he reached the village, the showdown had already begun, but he'd heard the deal that had been offered. The necklace for the nun. Foolishly Lilith had given up her only bargaining chip and before the trigger had been pulled, he knew the nun's fate was sealed.

At that moment he'd made his decision regarding the fate of the intruder and her thugs. A man had to pick a side.

"I promise you. They won't make it. Even if they do manage to land, they'll be lost in the jungle. I disabled the radio, as well."

"There are other villages. Not close, but…"

"On foot. In the jungle. In the middle of the night. Without the right skills they'll be some animal's feast before dawn."

She seemed to consider his conclusion but then she was shaking her head.

"I cannot take that chance."

"It's just a damn necklace," he said, irritated with her insistence. Hadn't he just avenged her friend? Hadn't he thwarted her enemies? Where were the thanks?

"No. I must go and find them. You need to help me."

Her urgency was palpable. So much that he was willing to bet it was more than just a damn necklace. Merciless destruction, cold-blooded elimination. All that for jewelry? No, he supposed there had to be more to the story. Tarak tried to summon a few reasons why he shouldn't see this through. They came easily enough.

One: his leg hurt.

Two: he needed to be concerned about his future and that meant finding out who had betrayed him in the jungles of Colombia.

Three: as hot as he was for the nymph, she was more

skittish around him than she was a leper. Which meant the likelihood of getting some action should he prove to be successful in his quest to retrieve the necklace was slim.

"Oh bother." He sighed, knowing himself too well. "Fine. Say please."

Her head tilted slightly to the right, a gesture he was coming to understand signaled her skepticism.

"Please," he repeated. "You're asking me to take off into the jungle after five armed men...."

"Four. One of them is dead."

Interesting. He'd seen a body at her feet during the standoff, but he hadn't seen what had happened before then. Was it possible his waif had actually taken one of the men down? Definitely interesting.

"Four men and one really badass woman. The least you could do is say please."

"Please," she whispered.

What a sucker he was.

Chapter 7

Together Lilith and Tarak made their way back to the village. The fires had either burned themselves out or had been put out by villagers. The monks had come down from the monastery to help, but it was too late. The destruction was almost complete. Smoke still filled the air, heavy and thick, as did the glow of the ashes. It almost looked like dawn even though it was still the middle of the night.

Lilith found Sister Joseph saying a prayer over Sister Peter's body, now covered with a blanket. But the blanket didn't cover the red stream that continued to seep out of her body and into the earth.

"I must leave, Sister. I will find her and she will pay. I promise."

Sister Joseph wiped a tear from her eye and shook her head. "The Lord said, vengeance is Mine."

"Don't worry. There will be enough left over for Him," Tarak said as he came to stand by Lilith. "We'll move out in a few hours just before dawn breaks."

"We can move now," Lilith said.

"Maybe you didn't hear me before. Through the jungle…in the middle of night…equals danger."

"Torches will be enough to keep the animals at bay."

He lifted his eyebrows high on his head. "You're not the nervous sort, are you? All right. But I'll need to go back to the monastery to get some…supplies. You'll need sturdy clothes and shoes."

Lilith nodded. She knew what she would need. "I am sorry I cannot stay with you during this time. I believe that Sister Peter's essence remains with us for a while longer. That we can talk to her and remind her of what she was to us so that her last thoughts before rebirth are good ones."

Sister Joseph nodded. "Our beliefs our different, but I, too, believe that if we speak to her somehow she will hear us. And you can think those good thoughts wherever you are, can't you?"

"Yes."

"Then do that," Sister Joseph told her. "I don't understand what happened. I don't know who that woman was or why she came to our village. Why she destroyed so much with so little reason. And I don't understand why you can't let her go. But I have lived long enough to recognize evil. I know that it comes in many forms. When you find it you must confront it. I suppose I can't fault you for wanting to chase her down and see that she doesn't commit more harm."

"Thank you."

"God bless you, child. And you," the sister said, pointing at Tarak. "You keep her safe."

"Yes, ma'am."

It took only minutes for Lilith to round up the supplies she needed. For nourishment and to save them from having to hunt, she took a bag of dried meat and an animal skin full of water. For clothes she tucked up the silk material between her legs and secured it at her waist to give her freedom of movement. Her sandals weren't the sturdiest shoes, but they were all she had and she'd managed well enough in them for years.

Her gloves as always were a necessity.

Waiting for Tarak frustrated her even though she knew there was no point in the emotion as she would not leave without him. It was almost a half an hour before Tarak found her in the center of the village. Returning from the monastery, he looked very different than he had earlier that night. Like Echo, his clothes reflected a new purpose. He wore black pants, a black shirt, heavy boots and a vest covered with many pockets. One she assumed held the knife, the others she suspected were for extra ammunition. Under each arm he'd holstered a gun. On his right arm he carried a backpack that looked stuffed to capacity. He removed one item from it then slung it back on his shoulder as if it weighed nothing.

For his strength, she thought. This was why she needed him. But more than that, a man of violence would understand a woman of violence. Echo was certainly that.

When he saw her efforts at preparation for their march into the jungle he frowned. "I tell you sturdy and you're in sandals and gloves. We're not going to a ball, you know."

Lilith looked at her covered hands. "The gloves are for your protection."

"My protection?"

Lilith needed to do this quickly, before they left. She would not risk losing him in the jungle because he'd made the stupid mistake of touching her.

"Come." She made Tarak follow her to where the body of the man who had touched her still lay. She pulled back the blanket that had been placed over him to show Tarak. "He touched me and died."

"I guessed as much. You hit him? Stabbed him?"

"No. One touch of my skin. That was all. It is…poisonous. I do not have time to explain. You must trust me. The woman that we are chasing is special, too. We are experiments. Tampered with genetically. Creatures of misplaced science. I do not know how and I do not care at this point. I need you to know that if you touch me you will die. Do you understand? I am untouchable."

Tarak thought back to that day when he'd stumbled upon her during her bath. The fear that he'd seen in her eyes. Not of being raped but of what might happen to him if he touched her. And that night when she'd come to his room when he was sick. She'd been summoned for a reason. He remembered the way his whole body had gone numb after a few drops of water on his lips. It was like nothing he'd ever felt before.

"That night. When I had the fever. You touched the water."

"Yes," she said. "A small dose can numb the body. I am called to help when we have to do amputations. To stop the pain. But direct contact will kill."

"I almost grabbed you several times out there in the jungle."

"I would not have let you. I am very skillful in avoiding people's touch. But now we must travel together. Sleep close. You must know to take precautions."

Tarak nodded. He wasn't certain he understood what the hell genetic tampering meant or how a woman came to have poisonous skin, but like Sister Joseph he'd seen enough in this world to know that stranger things were possible. Then there was the fact that his shot should have taken down the woman with the gun and it hadn't. He hit what he aimed at, always.

But what sealed his belief was that he had a gut-deep hunch that Lilith wouldn't lie. Certainly not about something that might hurt him. There was a purity about her soul that made him wonder if she even knew how to be deceitful. However, it was clear to him that with her purity apparently came an iron will.

Lilith was standing on the edge of the jungle armed with nothing more than silk gloves and a fire torch. "We must go. Each minute that passes they get farther away."

"All right. First let's see where we're going." Tarak used the receiver in his hand and punched in a code.

"What is that?"

"It's a GPS receiver. If the helicopter has a tracker, which most do now, I should be able to locate its direction. You didn't honestly think I was going to wander around in the jungle looking for a wrecked helicopter?"

"They would have headed south. It's where the nearest cities are."

"I can do better than south."

Once he located the blip, easy to find as it was the only one on his screen, he punched a few buttons and let the receiver return a location to him. "I've got them. Let's have at it then."

Tarak took a second torch and followed behind her. A few feet into the heavy foliage and he could no longer see the lingering fires of the village behind him. A few more and he could no longer hear the civilization they had left.

It was officially just the two of them against four armed thugs, a genetically altered woman and the jungle.

Tarak wasn't sure he liked their odds.

It didn't rain. It didn't pour. It deluged. Hour after hour of some of the hardest rain Tarak could imagine. Yet in front of him Lilith continued to walk without a stumble or a complaint. It appeared that Lilith was right.

The chopper had been heading south. Bomdila was the nearest city where one might find transport out of the province. It's where the thugs must have rented the helicopter in the first pace.

However, there was no way to know how far the chopper would take them as it continued to lose gas. Tarak and Lilith's only choice was to follow the dot and hope that eventually they could catch up with it. But even with the GPS, Tarak thought the odds of finding the helicopter were slim. It was the nature of the jungle to camouflage its denizens. Heavy foliage, fallen trees. They might be within a few kilometers of the Merry Murderer and her men and never find them.

Lilith wouldn't listen to him.

Hour after hour she forged ahead. Through the dark, over uneven terrain. With the sounds of animal calls closer than he would have liked dogging at their heels. She didn't stop when the sun came up. She didn't hesitate when the rain started to fall.

He wondered how far she might go before he put a stop to it. His bet was that she would go until her legs collapsed under her.

"Lilith, we must stop. We have to find shelter."

She turned around and shook her head. "We need to find higher ground. To see if we can see the remains of a wreck. You said we are getting closer."

The helicopter had stopped moving. He knew that much. "In this rain we could be standing over the damn thing and you still wouldn't see it."

"We must try."

"My leg, Lilith. I don't know how much farther I can go on my leg." It was a lie. He'd made it out of a Colombian jungle with a bullet still in it, but instinct told him the lie would work.

She stopped and turned around. He could see the concern in her eyes as her gaze fell to his leg.

"Of course. We will find shelter. Let me climb to get a vantage point."

He knew it. A soft touch. What in the hell was she doing out in the jungle searching for a killer? Better yet what was he doing here with her?

He watched as she made her way up a banyan tree, climbing it like a native to the forest. Considering the village where she lived, he imagined she was.

It was odd. Even with his eyes pinned to her as he watched her ascent, it was as if she became part of the landscape. Something about the nature of her skin seem to blend with her surroundings in a way that made him sure that if he took his eyes off her for a second, he would lose her amongst the flora. Staring at her, he could really only see the damn gloves.

"Tarak! Tarak! I see something. A curl of smoke to the east."

She shimmied down the tree and he couldn't help but linger on the sight of the wet silk sliding up her bare leg. Instantly an image of her without the bolt of silk reappeared in his mind.

All right. So it wasn't totally inconceivable that he

followed this woman into the jungle—a poisonous woman no less—because he had the hots for her. Pathetic, but not inconceivable.

Lilith jumped the remaining few feet to the ground and raced to where Tarak stood. He glanced down at his receiver.

"It's only another kilometer, two at most. You can wait here to rest your leg and I'll go…"

He agreed with her assessment. From where they were now it was only a kilometer and a half to the east. Unbelievably lucky. Or unbelievably unlucky. He wasn't sure. "You'll stay behind me."

"But…"

Tarak pulled his left gun out of its holster. "You'll stay behind me. I need to assess the situation before charging in. Do you understand?"

"Then give me the other gun."

"You want a gun?" he asked, incredulous. "Do you know how to shoot it?"

Lilith bristled at his tone. For most of last night and all of today he'd been trying to convince her that they would never find the crash site. Now that she had, he seemed ready to take over. She knew she had asked for his help, but she also knew that this was her mission. It was her responsibility to stop her sister. She would not be left behind.

He was speaking to her as if she were a simpleton. "I imagine you point it at the person you want to harm and you pull the trigger."

"I'll keep the guns. You concentrate on staying out of sight. If someone comes at you then I suppose you can…touch them."

Again Lilith wanted to argue, but again she reminded herself that she'd asked him to come along. She only hoped that the monks were right, that he was a warrior, because that was who she needed on this mission.

She thought back to the bullet that had bounced off Echo's shield. It would have been a direct hit. She needed to trust that he was good at what he did, to believe in what she'd already seen.

Besides, it wasn't in her nature to confront. After so long being controlled by her father, then her curse, she was a being of tolerance and humbleness. She worked hard. She helped the sick. She tried to do no harm.

Why this man's attitude toward her should bother her she couldn't say. But it did.

"Did you make a face at me?"

Had she? "It was not intentional."

"Has anyone ever told you you're beautiful when you're annoyed?"

Startled, it took a second before she could admit, "No."

"They should have."

He turned his back to her then and headed off in the direction she'd told him. She watched his leg, initially fearful of how painful the next kilometer might be for him and the setback it would cause toward his healing. Then she saw how he walked without any restriction of movement, not favoring the leg or showing any indication of pain at all and she suspected that he'd lied. Lied to get her to slow down even though she said she hadn't wanted to.

Lilith was sure that if he turned to look at her now, he would most definitely see another face.

As they neared their destination, Lilith pointed to the trail of smoke that was visible over the tree line. They could only be meters away from the crash site. Slowly Tarak covered his lips with his fingers to indicate silence from this point forward. Like an inhabitant of the jungle he slunk into the rhododendron bushes, barely shuffling them.

Lilith continued behind him, trying to mimic his grace, but she could hear the ruffle of flora trembling as she moved even over the torrential rain. Working harder to follow his model, she crouched low and stopped.

Through a break in the trees she could see the fallen helicopter tilted on its side. One of the blades was broken and the windshield appeared to be cracked.

But it wasn't empty. A figure sat in the pilot's seat. Maybe waiting for help to return?

Before Lilith could think to motion to Tarak in warning, she could see him slinking out of a thicket of green, moving along the ground like a snake waiting to jump up and attack the belly of the machine.

With a lightning-fast strike, he pulled open the pilot-side door, his gun already at the man's head. Lilith gasped, prepared for retaliation, but Tarak remained still. After a second he reached inside the helicopter and pulled the man out of the wreckage.

Lilith didn't have to see the large gash across the man's face to know he was dead. His open, unblinking eyes told their own story.

Sensing there was no threat, she moved from her hiding place and joined Tarak over the body.

"She left him."

"Yes," he confirmed. "Maybe he was already dead. Maybe he wasn't. I don't see that it would matter much to her."

"They took everything with them?"

Tarak leaned into the chopper and Lilith had the urge to sneak a peek over his shoulder, even though she knew such close contact was forbidden. The idea that Echo might have lost the necklace was less than improbable.

"It seems. Without the radio we know they couldn't have called for a pick up. That's good news."

"Why?"

"Because now there are only three goons left plus your friend."

"She's not my friend."

"I just meant…"

"She is my sister. Echo," Lilith explained. She couldn't say why she felt the need to tell him or how it impacted their mission. She only knew that withholding that information seemed wrong, especially when he'd already come so far for no other reason than that she had asked him.

"Really? This story should make for excellent entertainment over the campfire tonight."

"But we must be close. If we keep going…"

"We're not going anywhere until dawn. Don't you get it? They're on foot now, too. They're human—well, almost, I suppose. The rain will slow them like it has us. Plus, there are more of them, so they will move slower. We'll stay here, use the helicopter for shelter and then start out before first light." He paused. "You know I'm right."

She did. And she couldn't imagine why that irritated her so much.

"Good. We sit tight for a while. You have water and jerky that should get us through tonight. Tomorrow, I'll hunt for snakes."

"You have to know which snakes are edible. Some that are venomous are not fit to eat."

"Are you suggesting I don't know how to handle dangerous snakes?"

Lilith shrugged. She'd never been one to tell anyone anything, but she found herself snapping back, "I am telling you I know more about poison than you ever will."

"I'll take your word for it. Come on, we've got to get this body away from the crash site before it attracts some visitors we would rather not meet up with."

Lilith nodded. Working together, they pulled the heavy body as far away as Tarak thought reasonable and then covered it with brush and twigs. It wouldn't save the man from being dinner for some lucky animal, but at least some effort had been made to respect the dead.

When they returned to the chopper Tarak waited until

Lilith crawled into the passenger's seat and then carefully maneuvered himself into the pilot's seat. He could see the blood smeared on the windshield and dismissed it. He was too happy to be out of the rain for it to matter. As a man who had spent more time in the elements than he had in luxury surroundings he was surprised he even noticed the rain. But he had.

A sure sign he was getting soft.

Next to him, Lilith curled up into a small ball conscious, no doubt, of the size of their shelter. The space inside the chopper was tight. He could hear her breathing. Only he couldn't touch her. At all.

It was going to be a long night.

Chapter 8

She couldn't get comfortable in the small confines of the helicopter. He was too close. The rain continued to pound down. The noise was terrible off the inorganic material of the machine. Like an unending shower of tiny bullets. At least she was dry. That's what she tried to tell herself.

Only she could smell him.

Lilith shifted in the bucket seat again, looking for the farthest distance she could find. She had already determined it would be rude to move into one of the seats in back. Not that another few inches would make much difference. She was sure she would smell him from back there, too.

"Can you please stop fidgeting?"

His eyes were closed, his arms crossed loosely over his stomach. He looked very relaxed within his space. That plus the even rise and fall of his chest, which she had watched for what felt like hours, almost made her believe him to be asleep.

Almost.

But she knew that even as he rested he was still alert. She could practically feel his senses filtering out the extraneous data. The sound of the rain. The creaking of the trees as they bent under the relentless pressure. Searching all of it for the anomalies that would signal danger. It was that invisible tension keeping her up.

That and his smell.

"I do not fidget." It was silly to be offended, but she was. Fidgeting made her sound like a young child.

He tilted his head in her direction. A single eye popped open. "I hate to break this to you, Lilly. But you fidget."

"That is not my name."

"Lilly? No, it isn't. But I'm having a difficult time calling you Lilith."

"Why?"

"Do you know where it comes from? The origination of the name?"

Lilith nodded. "My father." She paused over the word. Did she even need to call him that anymore? "The man who sired me told me that Lilith spawned monsters." It was such an awful image for a child to grow up with. She could see now he intended it that way. Curiously she wondered who was responsible for naming her. It certainly wasn't a traditional Nepalese name. It must have come from Jackie. No doubt the woman had found a perverse humor in the name. Or maybe it was her ironic way of naming Lilith after herself.

"Okay, you know she didn't actually… I mean that she's a myth."

"You think because of where I live that I am not sophisticated about the world. I have learned many things from the monks and the nuns. I have studied very hard. I am not stupid."

"Hackles down, Lilly. I wasn't trying to offend. Just trying to get a sense of where you come from…philosophically that is."

"I am a Buddhist."

"The nuns couldn't convert you?"

Lilith thought of Sister Joseph and it made her smile. "They tried."

"I'm sure. Perfect setup for them actually. You're already half nun. You believe in helping people. You're obviously self-sacrificing. No worries about the chastity issue because well, you're deadly."

Lilith bristled. It wasn't so much the remark, but his tone. He wasn't trying to insult her. Instead she believed he was poking fun at her. "You are mocking me," she accused. "Or do you think I am lying? If I could demonstrate I would. Unfortunately for you, you would not live to see the results."

Tarak shrugged. "Of course I do not think you are lying. You are far too serious for that, Lilly. But tell me how you learned of this. How does someone come to realize that their touch is literally poison?"

"My mother was dead. As a child I asked why. My father told me it was because I killed her as she gave birth to me. As well as the doctor who delivered me. Then as a young woman my uncle tried to… He wanted me for a wife. He wanted to…touch me. You understand?"

"Sadly, yes."

"He died, too. My father said it was because I was cursed. Now I know better."

"Do you?"

"Yes. I was not cursed. I was made. There is a difference."

"And if I reached over and crossed the space separating us and touched your cheek or your lips or your shoulder…"

Lilith met his gaze directly. "You would die." She watched sadness seep into his eyes. "You pity me. Please do not."

Then he snorted and turned away from her. "Pity you? Hell, I pity myself. First time in a long time I've been in close quarters with a woman I want with nothing better to do to pass the time and she's off-limits. Trust me, if anyone is the victim in this scenario it's me."

She watched him close his eyes and thought that she would let his words pass unnoticed, but he was right. For the first time she was alone with a man other than a relative, a leper or an abstinent monk. She found herself curious.

"Why does a man want a woman?"

"Oh, this should get interesting." Again Tarak shifted so that he was facing her. "I have no good answer for that, Lilly. We just do."

"And you take what you want. Like my uncle tried to do."

"Your uncle sounds like a sick man. Not all men take. Sometimes we can't stop the wanting. But we can always stop the taking."

"Will it go away? This wanting, now that you know you cannot have me."

He closed his eyes and sighed deeply. "No. In fact, it is probably only going to get worse the more I get to know you. First, I wanted you because of your body. The color and shape of it. The way your skin shines makes me yearn to touch it. Then, I wanted you more when I saw you try to fight your sister even after the blow you had been dealt by the loss of your friend. Then, even more when you asked me to help you because I knew it was hard for you, but you did it anyway. These things make me want you."

"Fighting? Asking for help?" It didn't make any sense to her why those things would attract a man.

"Courage and persistence. They happen to be two of my favorite traits. So will it go away? Probably not. Would I ever take you…"

"You cannot," she insisted.

"Lilly, if your skin was made out of pure silk rather than poison I still wouldn't take you unless you wanted me to."

"Oh."

Again, Tarak rolled away and once more closed his eyes. "Now tell me," he said casually. "Why do you want me?"

"I do not know," Lilith answered honestly. It didn't occur to her to be coy. There was no reason for it. Truth had no impact on the reality of their situation. "I have never felt this before. It is like a tug in the center of my body. I think it has to do with your smell."

He chuckled and the sound made her smile. "Go to sleep. They'll be moving fast tomorrow. We'll need to move faster if we're to catch up. We can't do that if we're not rested."

She tried to do as he asked, but sleep seemed so elusive. Over and over again she could see Echo holding the gun to Sister Peter's head. She could see the anger and the terror in the nun's eyes and then nothing. Just a slumping of the body that signaled instant and complete death. Then Echo had just let her go.

Revenge wasn't something Lilith had ever believed in until now. The heat of it was something that she couldn't ignore. It gave her power even though she knew that it wasn't the kind of power that she wanted. This journey she was on would test her in ways that she knew she hadn't been tested before.

The frightening part was that Lilith had no idea how she would fare.

The next morning Tarak lifted his head, startled that he'd let himself fall so deeply into sleep. He was still recovering and his body hadn't responded as well to the ten-hour trek the day before as he would have liked. Was it possible that he was getting old?

Old before his thirtieth birthday?

No. Definitely not possible. But he couldn't deny the life he'd led had hardened him. Aged him. Beaten him down and spit him out on occasion. There was always another fight. Another battle. Another mission.

There was never just peace. In his heart he knew that's what had sent him back to his mother's people. He'd needed to rest his body, yes, but he had also needed to rest his soul.

For a brief second he wondered what his parents would have thought of his retreat. His father would have frowned. Peace was for the weak. His mother would have said nothing to contradict his father but she would have been glad that for a short time he was not in danger.

Or at least he hadn't been in danger until he met Lilith.

Lilith. Lilly. Yes, definitely Lilly.

Shaking off the strange melancholy that always accompanied thoughts of his parents, Tarak turned and saw that his copilot was already up and gone. Fearing she might have foolishly gone after the enemy on her own, he opened the door to the helicopter and maneuvered himself out onto the overturned tree that it had crashed on.

"Stop. Do not move any farther."

Unable to heed the warning, he turned to his left, in the direction of the voice, and saw her standing rather calmly just beyond a bush.

Calmly considering she was facing off against a full-size male tiger.

Tarak quickly swallowed his shout. Exciting the animal would do no good. Five meters in either direction, the tiger stood motionless between them. Then a slow turn of the head indicated the beast was aware of Tarak's presence behind him. A slow turn back to Lilith let Tarak know that the animal didn't consider him a threat.

"Beautiful," Tarak whispered. And he was. Orange like he'd never seen before with inky-black and snow-white stripes. The tiger resonated power. "I'm sorry I have to do this."

He reached for the gun in his holster, but Lilith held up her hand.

"There is no need to shoot him."

"He could attack at any second. If I wait until he makes his move you will already be dead."

"He is not in an attack position. His back is not arched. His tail is not down. And truly I am not a large enough prey to entice him. He wants a deer or a fat wild boar. Besides, I think he can sense I would not taste very good."

Tarak remained still. As did Lilith and the animal. "What about me?" he half joked.

"You, he would eat."

"Of course."

"But as I said, he is not interested in hunting today. Go now," she urged the beast gently. "Find your meal elsewhere."

As if the tiger understood her language, he turned and

slowly walked off into the forest. After five more seconds Tarak could finally breathe.

"I thought they were all on preserves."

"Most are. But some still roam wild. And despite their low numbers, people still come to kill them for sport. I could not let you shoot it as long as I knew there was no threat. The smell of the body we covered might have attracted him. They usually keep their distance from people."

"No threat," Tarak puffed. "I've never been so close to a deadly animal like that in my life. It was facing you, but you had the presence of mind to assess the threat level?"

To that, she simply shrugged. "I have washed already and filled my water supply. There is a stream not too far east. Once you are ready we can be on our way."

"Our best chance is to head for the river and follow it south until we find civilization." Tarak pulled his backpack out of the helicopter and slung it over his shoulders.

"That is the path Echo and her men will take."

"Right. We're following them, remember? Big ugly necklace. You want it back."

Lilith shook her head slightly. "I meant to say, if we cut through the jungle heading southwest for a time, we could make up ground on them."

"Or lose it, depending on how difficult the terrain is and what we run into."

"Yes," she allowed. "Or lose it. Echo will not be moving slowly. She will want to get to where she needs to be as fast as she can."

"And where is that? Ultimately?"

"I do not know. My guess would be first to Bomdila as we suspected. That's about two hundred kilometers from where we are now. If she makes it there she can find transportation. From there she will want an even bigger city. One with an airport that has planes to everywhere in the world."

Tarak considered asking why Lilith was so certain that would be the case, but decided there would be more than enough time for questions later. Now they needed to set a course.

"New Delhi fits the bill. And it's closer than Calcutta," Tarak concluded. "If she makes it there, we'll never find her. We'll have to go on as if she's headed to Bomdila first and trust that we're right."

"We found the helicopter."

"With a tracker and a GPS receiver. Neither one of which are of use anymore."

He didn't bother to point out that trying to take the same general direction and hoping to find four people in a jungle that spanned over ten thousand square kilometers wasn't going to be easy.

"Right," he decided. "We'll cut through the jungle heading southwest and hope she sticks to the water. If she finds a village with a boat or a car…"

"She won't. There are few cars and fewer powered boats in these villages. And the people are very suspicious. Outsiders are not welcomed. The only foreigners they see are tourists out for sport. It is the same with people who come to our village to see the monastery. They are not trusted."

"We're talking at least another two, probably three, days on foot."

"I know. Will you be able to walk for so long?"

He tried not to let her innocent question prick his male pride. "I'll manage," he said dryly.

"Then we should go."

"I hate India in the springtime!" Echo sang out to the trees above her. "I hate India in the fall. I hate India, oh why do I hate India, because… I'm stuck in this hellish jungle with a bunch of incompetents who couldn't check the damn fuel line."

Echo chuckled at her little joke. Rolf turned around but was smart enough not to say anything.

"Actually, I have to give that girl credit. Cutting the fuel line. Priceless. How the hell did she even know what a fuel line was? Is it possible that I misjudged her? Maybe she wasn't some village half-wit. Maybe it was all a scam to throw me off. No, not possible," Echo said, talking herself out of her paranoid conclusions. "I do know one thing—I should have killed her when I had the chance."

"If we stick to the river's edge we should eventually find a village. Hopefully one with a car," Rolf said.

"Right." Echo snorted. "Lots of cars in this part of India. Just keep walking and keep your mouth shut. And get me the hell out of this jungle. I have a world to conquer."

"Do you think she'll follow us?"

Echo glanced behind her at Kent, who was bringing up the rear. "Worried she might want to reach out and touch you?"

"I would like to know if it's a possibility. Yeah."

"She did mess with my helicopter. Would she have the balls to chase me through the jungle to get her precious necklace back?" Echo smiled. "If only I could be lucky enough to have a chance to meet up with dear sis one more time. Don't worry. If she does come for us I'll know it."

"How?"

"I'll know it," Echo insisted through clenched teeth. "And this time I won't be so nice."

Chapter 9

"How is your leg?"

Lilith focused on the appendage even as Tarak hacked his way through the heavy bush in front of them with a machete he'd stowed in his backpack. When she asked what else he'd brought with him besides his guns, the GPS receiver and the canteen that he'd filled by the river, he simply stated that he had everything he needed. It was a very large backpack.

"Stop asking about my leg."

"If you need us to go slower I can…"

Tarak stopped and faced her. "If you finish that sentence I'm going to turn you over my knee and spank you. I'm fine."

Lilith knew it was an empty threat. But she also knew

enough about male pride from her father and the monks to know that she probably shouldn't be offering to slow down. Although if he was too lame to help her when she confronted Echo that wouldn't do her much good, either. Someone would have to explain to her why men could be so stubborn about their pride.

Night was beginning to fall, but they had decided to press on with the torches for a little longer. The hike during the day hadn't been too difficult. The rain had picked up in the afternoon, but had finally stopped. For the most part it had been uneventful and they'd managed to find some wild fruit that they could eat along the way.

"We do have to watch for leopards," she said. "They will hunt at night. Unlike the tiger we encountered they will find our size more to their liking."

"But you said the tiger sensed that you wouldn't taste very good. Are you telling me leopards aren't as discriminating?"

"No, I'm reminding you that while I might be safe you are still vulnerable. My guess is you would taste very good."

Again Tarak stopped in his tracks. He looked at her with an expression she didn't understand. "You don't realize what you just said, do you?"

"I was commenting on your vulnerability."

"Right." He sighed. "I wish you would stop worrying about me so much. I'll have you know I'm rather competent at what I do. This isn't the first time I've been in a jungle."

His face was lit by the torch he carried. She could see the sharp features that she was coming to know very well. This morning she'd watched him sleep for almost an hour until the need to reach over and touch him became so strong that she'd been forced to leave the helicopter. It had been foolish to wander off as far as she had. Despite what she told him she was lucky the tiger hadn't attacked. They both were.

But she had needed to…get away. It wasn't a need she could explain, only one that she could act on. Looking at him now, a part of her knew that the wisest course of action would be to have as little communication with him as possible. He was here to help her track down Echo and to retrieve the necklace. She was certain that knowing him beyond that would make the tug worse. Just like he had suggested last night. There were already things about him that were compelling to her. The sound of his laugh for one. The way he called her Lilly.

All of those tiny snippets were making her feel more urgent. It was possibly the strangest sensation she'd ever known. She couldn't stop herself.

"What do you do?" When he didn't answer immediately, Lilith added, "I know you are a man of violence. This is why I asked for your help. You do not have to lie to me."

"I wasn't planning on it. What I do is complicated."

"Why?"

He made a sound but it wasn't humorous. "I work for governments. I track down bad people. Bad people whom people in government want to stop from doing more bad things."

"An assassin." She tried to keep the judgment from her voice, but based on the way he looked at her she knew she hadn't.

"No. Not just an assassin. I don't always kill."

"But you have."

"Yes," he said. "Does that bother you? That I'm like your sister in that respect?"

"I have killed, too. You are like me in that respect."

"You have killed for defense. It is different. But you should know that I am not like your sister."

"I know. I would not have sought your help otherwise."

"Are you going to tell me about her?"

He lifted his hand and slashed through a heavy leaf. She saw him push it away and then he stopped. His arm dropping heavily to his side.

"Is it a snake?"

"No. It's a clear patch with a few strong surrounding trees. I think we should bunker down here. It's getting darker and I don't want to travel too much farther when I can't see what I'm hacking."

"But Echo," Lilith protested.

"They'll have to stop, too, Lilly. Look, we could be in front of her now for all we know. Or behind her. Or completely off course."

"You said earlier, though…"

He nodded and sighed. "Yes, I know. We're heading southwest as planned. That's great. I'm just telling you our chances of bumping into her in the middle of this jungle are slim. We'll do our best, but for now I'm not taking any more risks than we need to. This is a secluded spot. We'll set up the torches and pitch a tent."

"A tent."

Tarak rolled the backpack off his shoulders and dropped it in the patch of mossy grass. He stomped over a large area, checking for snakes, and when he was satisfied he unzipped his pack.

"I told you I had everything we needed. I know how to travel in a jungle when I'm doing it on foot. Last night we could use the helicopter. Tonight we'll use this."

She watched as he pulled from the pack a neatly folded square that after a few unfolds sprang up into a small shelter.

For one person it would be comfortable. For two— tight. "I cannot sleep in that tent with you."

"Can't or won't?"

The question confused her. "Both. It would be too risky. The slightest movement and I could touch you without realizing it."

Tarak nodded slowly. "I'll improvise. In the meantime you can use this to make a campfire."

He dug once more into his pack and tossed her a metal device with a long metal tube and a trigger. When she clicked it, fire came out of the nozzle. Fascinated, she clicked it a few more times. "It almost seems like cheating."

Tarak laughed and she found herself smiling as a result

of the sound. Together they went about their separate chores. Lilith made a central fire and set each torch to the east and west of the clearing. Tarak cut open the bottom of the tent, then laid out a tarp underneath it. With some sticks, he secured the newly expanded tent so that while it was more open to the elements it would provide shelter from the rain.

"There," he said when he finished. "We'll be safe enough under that."

Still Lilith was skeptical. "I'll sleep under the bottom tarp."

"The bugs will eat you alive."

"Better than me killing you."

Since he obviously couldn't argue with that they settled down into their makeshift camp. Having previously eaten, they simply finished the water and waited for time to pass before sleep claimed them.

Lilith stared up at the tent top and listened to the even breathing next to her. Just as it had been the previous night, she was reminded of the strange sensation that she felt whenever she was so close to him. She wondered if it would have been like this with any man who had come to her aid. Certainly she'd never felt such a thing for one of the villagers or the monks.

"I think it might be your face, as well," she said softly, wondering if he would even understand that she was answering a question from the night before. "You are what some women in my village would call handsome. It's pleasing."

"Thank you. I think," he added. "I imagine you are referring to your attraction to me. You shouldn't let it worry you, Lilly. It's a natural thing between men and women."

"There is nothing natural about me." It was a fact and not meant to sound as bitter as Lilith imagined it sounded.

"No, there isn't." She could feel him shift above the tarp. She tugged on it to make sure it didn't pull away from her leaving any skin revealed. She still wore her silk material and the gloves but she knew there were patches of skin exposed. She knew that because the bugs had found them.

"You didn't answer me earlier. Tell me about your sister."

"I told you everything. We were experiments. We were made to have skills, but something must have gone wrong. At least with me. Surely no one would have intentionally made me this way."

"Not unless someone was breeding a lethal assassin."

Lilith shifted under the tarp. "Sadly, that is not unlikely given the nature of who my mother was."

"And who is that exactly?"

"I knew her as Jackie Webb. A philanthropist. Then she died and a courier was sent telling me of her death and telling me of my past."

Lilith thought it was enough information. She couldn't say that she didn't trust him with the rest. She was trusting him with her life. But instinct told her the less said about the files the better. She could tell herself it was for the same reason she hadn't wanted to tell

Sister Peter about the information she'd learned. Because she didn't want him to be a potential target.

But that wasn't true.

Tarak said he worked for governments. Many of the people in those files were government leaders. Men and women whom he'd probably served at some point, whom he might have to serve again in the future. He didn't need to know how corruptible they were. No one should ever be that disillusioned.

She comforted herself that her omission of the truth was for his own good.

In the dark quiet she could feel his scrutiny. His head was propped up on his hand as he stared down into her face, seeing what, she wasn't sure as the small fire gave off only flickers of light.

"You're not a very clever liar."

It was a fact. "It is because I do not do it very often."

"Your mother gave you more than your past. More than a sister, as well."

"What she gave me doesn't matter. Stopping my sister does."

"Stopping her from doing what?"

"You saw what she did to Sister Peter."

She let her eyes drift to his face and saw him nod slowly. "I did. And it was ruthless. But she did it with a very specific intent. What's in the necklace?"

"It was what my mother left me. I want it back." Unclever liars did best by sticking to the truth.

"Fine," he said, eventually rolling onto his back. "You

don't want to tell me what's in the necklace. Let me tell you then. A woman named Jackie Webb somehow masterminded the biological engineering of at least two offspring. One has altered skin chemistry, the other can stop bullets. I know this because I'm a very good shot. Jackie's dead, but she manages to get off a note to you along with a necklace and a computer. I saw the laptop you tried to foist off on sis—nice try, by the way."

"It did not work."

"Then Echo shows up in all her glorious madness. She burns your village and kills a nun, all for the family jewels. I don't think so. You know what I do think?"

"You seem quite talkative this night," Lilith snipped, irritated with his flawless logic. "I imagine you are going to tell me even if I do not want to hear it."

"She stings and bites," Tarak noted. "I think the secret to this genetic process is somehow in the necklace. Information like that…it's scary to think what a woman like Echo would do with it."

Lilith hadn't considered that, but it was probably true. She hadn't gone so deep into the files after quickly being disgusted by what she read, but she imagined there was more than blackmail. The idea of another child, an innocent being, suffering her fate doubled her determination to stop Echo.

"Now you understand why we must stop her."

"I never doubted it. Mostly because I never doubted you. I just wanted you to tell me."

"Why? If you already knew."

"I needed to know that you trusted me. No, that's not true. I already do know. I just wanted you to admit it."

"Why?"

"Because it's part of the tug. Here we are in the middle of the jungle. You told me that what Echo has is of great value. I could kill you and move faster on my own. Then take her out and have the necklace all to myself."

Lilith shifted under the tarp. "But you won't. I know that you won't."

"You're right. But how do you know it?" he pressed. "You've only known me a handful of hours. I could be anyone."

"I cannot say. I feel it inside."

"Exactly. That's what I wanted you to admit. You feel me. You trust me. It's part of the tug. Do you understand?"

Lilith sighed and relaxed more now that she understood what he wanted from her. "Yes. I knew a man I called my father my whole life. I shared a home with him. I worked beside him. Every day. I never knew him."

"It can happen that way. People can not know the person sleeping next to them after a lifetime. Or know intimately the person they just met. It's what makes us so complex. I'm glad to know that I wasn't alone in my feelings."

"But these feelings are useless," Lilith insisted, frustrated. "You know nothing can come of it. It's impossible."

"Impossible," Tarak murmured as he settled on his back and tried to get as comfortable as he could. "I'm not a big believer in impossible. They told me it would be impossible to find the terrorists that blew up my father and my mother along with him. But I did. I found them and I killed them. Impossible is what makes me tick. Never doubt it."

Lilith had no answer for that. But if she could have she would have reached out and touched his shoulder and offered him comfort. Because she couldn't she turned on her side and hoped that the bugs would leave her some of her skin.

Spitefully she hoped they didn't survive the feast.

Tarak sat up slowly, letting his body adjust to the position. It was at least an hour until dawn but the night was fading. It must have been the sounds of the jungle waking up that alerted him to the arrival of morning.

For a moment he took stock of the situation. Both torches were no more than red husks, and the fire, too, had dwindled to embers, but fortunately there were no predators around looking for an easy meal this morning.

He glanced down at his tent mate and saw the curve of her face as it was turned away slightly from him. So beautiful. And different, too, in this light. Her skin seemed milky, not quite as shiny. As if the sheen that could be so compelling had diminished overnight.

Overnight while she slept.

As the thought rattled around in his head, he watched as she stirred and slowly woke. As she sat up, the tarp fell from her shoulders. Glimpses of skin were exposed through the mock sari and he could see that those patches had also lost that strange luminescent quality.

Crawling out from under the tent, he rummaged around on the ground.

"What are you doing?"

"A test," he said as he found a small, sharp rock. "Stand up."

Lilith hesitated, but after he motioned to her, she followed his lead. She stood in front of him trying to adjust the silk strips around the exposed areas of her skin, but he held up a hand to stop her.

"No. Leave your right shoulder exposed."

"If this is some kind of game…"

Tarak didn't bother answering. He took a step back and flung the rock with little force in the direction of her shoulder. It bounced off and he saw her wince. Almost instantly her skin tone changed.

"What are you doing? Was there a bug?"

"Interesting."

"Have you gone mad?" she snapped, rubbing the offended shoulder. "Is the strain of the journey affecting you?"

"I'll explain on the way. Let's break camp down. We need to keep moving if we hope to have a chance of finding our needle in the haystack."

"We'll find them. Just like we found the helicopter."

Tarak snorted. "If only your friend had a tracking device built inside of her then sure… Oh shit. Of course. How could I have been so stupid? No wait, in my defense this is your fault. You should have told me about the damn necklace right from the start."

"I do not understand."

Tarak didn't waste time explaining. He simply dug his GPS receiver out of his backpack and started making adjustments to look for other signals in the area. If he was right, in this area of Arunachal Pradesh so scarcely populated there wouldn't be many. Maybe a few tour guides with cell phones. Which meant the odds he would find more than one signal moving in the direction they had already anticipated were less than slim.

He saw the beep flash on his screen and calculated that they were about three kilometers southwest of their target.

"Smile," he murmured. "You're on radar."

Chapter 10

Lilith moved as close as she dared and watched a tiny beep in the lower half of the screen.

"You think that is Echo?"

"Pretty good bet, yes. She's heading south along the path of the river, just as we figured she would."

"But how?"

"The necklace. Given the information it contains I would have been more surprised if your mother hadn't put a tracker inside it. My GPS receiver has been modified in a way that allows me to pick up anything giving off a signal. Given where we are, I'm about eighty percent certain that dot is your sister."

"Please do not call her my sister. It bothers me." It was a silly request, but she didn't feel guilty for making it. That she was connected by blood to two women who were capable of such evil did not sit well with her. She knew from her teachings with the monks that children could not credit everything to their parents, nor could they assign all blame. A child eventually had to make his or her own way and be responsible for his or her own actions.

Those lessons had helped her to overcome the pain of being an unwanted child and helped her to put her father and his actions behind her. Now she would have to do the same with Jackie and with Echo.

It seemed unfair that one child should be cursed with such a family tree and more unfair that she would never have a chance to have her own family. A man who would love her. A child she would love. A chance to correct the mistakes that had been made by the generation before her in a way that would offer balance to the universe. An act of goodness for every evil that had been done.

It was how she would have tried to raise her children.

Sadness descended on her and she had to concentrate hard to shake it off. Now wasn't the time to think about what she'd lost. No, she would never be able to make up for what Jackie had done by bringing good people into this world, but she could continue to do good work herself. She had an opportunity to stop Echo from doing more harm. If she succeeded then that would have to be her legacy.

Thanks to Tarăk, they now knew where Echo was.

"We should go now."

"Not so fast. We're not that far behind her, believe it or not. Your idea of cutting through the jungle worked."

"Then why are we waiting? We should hurry to reach her and…stop her."

"And exactly how do you propose that we do that? I can't shoot her. We need to think before we act."

Lilith nodded. He was right. In her defense, she had no mind for strategy when it came to capturing an opponent. Everything that had happened to her since the moment the first helicopter had arrived was new territory. She was in the dark, but that was why she had brought Tarak with her. He was her torch.

"We'll follow her at a distance," he said. "Maybe find some way to lure her men away from her and take them down individually. Eventually, come nightfall, she'll have to stop to make camp again. We'll have a better chance of catching her unawares then."

"Yes, that is logical," Lilith conceded.

"This is what I do," he reminded her.

Lilith nodded and then proceeded to roll up the tarp she had slept under. Together they worked quickly to break down the camp. The torches were spent and they had brought no extra supply of oil to keep them lit, so they were left behind. Tarak shouldered his backpack but kept the GPS receiver in his hand.

Lilith took his machete and led the way for a while, hacking through heavy leaves and bushes to create a path for them. They were close. She could feel it. And because they were she found her adrenaline easily giving her the strength she needed to move faster and work harder.

"You never told me why you threw that rock at me," Lilith said after she made a slice through a heavy plant. "It hurt."

"Sorry about that," Tarak said from behind her. "I was conducting a little test."

"A test? I do not understand."

"Have you noticed that your skin changes at different times of the day?"

Lilith glanced down at her covered hand. She couldn't see much of her skin ever because of the coverings she wore. At night when she was alone and comfortable enough to remove her robes and gloves it was always dark.

"No, I have never noticed any particular changes. I don't often see my skin as it's usually draped in silk. In what way does it change?"

"The look of it. Sometimes it's as if it shimmers. Glows. Something. Other times it's a natural, soft color. Like anyone else's skin."

Again Lilith glanced down at herself. She searched for and found a patch of skin exposed on her upper arm. To her it looked like her skin. She didn't see any difference. "I'm afraid the jungle has affected your mind and your sight it seems."

"No, I'm pretty sure I'm right. When you were sleeping there was no sheen. But when I threw the rock and hit you, instantly your skin started to glow again. It makes perfect sense."

"It makes no sense at all."

"Don't you see? It's a defense mechanism. The poison. And, as strange as this may sound, it's not all that unusual."

Lilith whacked at another leaf with particular force and paused as a rat snake slithered down the branch off the high plant and out of her path.

"You are saying that this condition is not unusual when I have told you that I was nothing more than a genetic experiment. Surely there are not more people out there like me."

"Unusual in a person, yes," he agreed. "Not in nature, though. There are highly poisonous frogs in South America. You've never been there but they have jungles much like this. These tiny frogs can be more deadly than a viper or a cobra. But it's not as if they are predators. They're too small. The poison is simply a defense mechanism for the frog against those that would attack it. And the sheen on their skin lets their natural enemies know that they are armed."

"You think I am related to a frog?" She knew he didn't mean it as such but she had a hard time not being offended.

"I think, Lilly, that your poison is similar. When you slept it receded, but when you were threatened it returned. Think about it. When you've killed? What were the circumstances leading up to it?"

Visions of her uncle attacking her came to mind. Then other visions of the village on fire. The man who slapped her cheek. Yes, they were times of stress and fear. But there had been other times. "I killed as a helpless baby."

"During childbirth," Tarak pointed out. "People often

talk about how stressful it is on the mother, but I imagine there is a fair amount of stress going on in the womb as a child makes that journey from darkness to light."

"Also, when I've been called to help the wounded or the suffering. I've been able to touch the water and turn it into medicine."

"Seeing someone suffering is a cause for stress. Especially with someone like you who feels so much. Look, Lilly, I can't know absolutely, but I think you need to consider that what you can do is more under your control than you believe."

She stopped and let the machete drop to her side. The idea of what he was saying overwhelmed her. Control. It was unthinkable. Impossible. To control her curse would mean…everything. But it wasn't possible, was it? She would have known. Surely at some point she would have realized.

But how? How could she have known? When she'd accepted for so long that she was untouchable in every way. All the time.

Tarak came up behind her and took the knife out of her hand, dangerously close to brushing against her as he did. Instantly Lilith jumped away.

"Are you trying to prove your theory by risking your life?" she asked, breathing heavily. Whether it was from the exertion of the trek or his surprising hypothesis she wasn't sure.

"No," Tarak said. "Now isn't the time for that. But I want you to think about it. Defense mechanisms are unconscious reactions. Like fight or flight. However, once you understand how you react when threatened that's one step toward taking control of your actions. Eventually your conscious mind can override your unconscious reactions. It just takes practice."

His words almost hurt. Desperately she wanted him to stop talking because with everything he said that made sense her heart bled. What he was doing was offering her hope. Planting a seed in her mind to suggest that she may not have to be isolated for the rest of her life.

Maybe he thought he was doing a good thing. But what if he was wrong?

What if he is right?

Lilith rejected the dangerous whisper from deep inside her soul where her most cherished wishes lived. She'd lived too long knowing exactly how deadly she was to anyone around her. To suggest otherwise was treacherous as well as foolish. His motive, then, had to be less noble.

"I believe you are saying this because you want to touch me. Even though you know you cannot."

He smiled then and it transformed his face from serious to charming. Lilith would have sworn she didn't know what charm was other than a word she had learned while practicing English. Now she understood it completely.

"While that would be a nice perk, I can assure you my survival instinct is stronger than my desire for you. Not by much, but enough. At least for now. I'm not saying this to upset you, Lilly. I'm saying it because, as unnatural as you think you are, Nature decided to let you live. If you look around this planet there are creatures filled with poison. Plants, flowers, bugs, frogs, snakes. In each case the poison exists for a reason. It is only logical that yours does, as well."

Tarak continued to walk then, the machete now in his hand as he took over the task of clearing a path for them.

His words filled her head in a way that made it hurt. She couldn't deny their veracity no matter how much she wanted to. How strange to think of herself as an anomaly all her life when really she was part of a different family. A natural family.

It was sometime later that Tarak craned his neck over his shoulder to smile at her, his teeth flashing white against the heavy green backdrop.

"Oh, and, Lilly," he said casually. "I should also add that all those species I mentioned manage to find a way to mate."

Charm. Yes, now she understood it and why people apparently had a hard time resisting it.

"Where the hell are we?" The humidity was thick in the air, signaling another downpour. The mere idea of more rain was enough to irritate every nerve in Echo's body.

Rolf looked up from his GPS receiver and sighed. "We've still got over a hundred kilometers to go. Maybe another day on foot."

"But this is boring!" Echo shouted. "I need to be doing more than slugging through this damn country." She clutched the necklace that dangled from her neck and felt it bite into her hand the more she squeezed it. The pain made her feel better as it was less boring than walking.

"Once we find transportation we'll be out of here soon enough," Kent reminded her. "Unless you have a better idea, we're stuck walking."

Echo's eyes thinned to slits. She imagined slitting Kent's throat with the blade she kept attached to her ankle and watching his expression of stunned horror as his life faded away. That definitely wouldn't be boring. She might have done it, too, just to set an example that she wasn't someone the men should feel free to converse with, if it hadn't been for the fact that she might need him still.

The first drop hit her face and she groaned. Soon the sky opened up and in seconds she was drenched.

"Oh, Mummy, there are so many things I will never forgive you for, but forcing me to come to this forsaken place is definitely one of them," she muttered to the sky. Then she laughed and looked down at the ground and laughed even harder. "Sorry. Wrong direction."

"We should think about making camp soon," Rolf suggested. "We've only got another hour of light. If we can find some dry wood now and keep it dry, when the rain stops we'll at least be able to have a fire."

"Fine," Echo relented. "How far inland from the river are we?"

"About two kilometers," Rolf reported.

Echo had sent him out a few times during their trek to search for any trace of civilization as well as to keep his eyes open for anyone who might be following. While Echo thought the possibility remote, she wasn't taking any chances.

"We'll need to cross it eventually to stay on course," he continued. "I saw a rope bridge, but it's back a few kilometers."

"I'm not going backward," Echo insisted. "We'll swim across if we have to."

Rolf opened his mouth to protest, but one look from Echo was enough to silence him.

"Go find some wood that isn't drenched. And while you're out there find me something to eat. I'm getting tired of fruit. Be manly men, won't you, and kill something. I have a hankering for some meat."

"They've stopped," Tarak noted as he continued to stare at the blip.

He showed the GPS receiver to Lilith but it wasn't much more to her than a dot on a small screen.

"The necklace hasn't moved for at least a half hour," he said. "No doubt they didn't want to continue on in the rain. A good sign."

"Why?"

"It means they feel comfortable enough to stop. They don't suspect that anyone could be following, which will give us the advantage of surprise when we move."

"Tonight?" Lilith asked, both fearful and determined that the time had come to take back what was hers.

"Tonight," Tarak confirmed. "We're about three kilometers back. We'll want to get closer, but not too close. Her men will set up a periphery that they'll secure with regular watches."

"That seems excessive if they do not think they are being followed."

Tarak shrugged. "These men are soldiers. Hired or not. They'll fall back on their training, which is to be watchful and on guard at all times. Even if not directed to do so by Echo."

Lilith nodded. "We'll need a plan." She didn't have to be a soldier to know that much was a given. She thought about what approach she might take and other than attempting to sneak by Echo's men and steal the necklace she didn't have many ideas. And if Echo was wearing the necklace, as Lilith had done, and could erect her force field to prevent Lilith from touching her, then that idea wasn't feasible.

Tarak dropped to his haunches. He found a stick and began to draw lines in the mud. Lilith sank to her knees and studied his crude map. Not for the first time, she silently praised herself for having the fore-thought to know she would need Tarak on this mission. She'd seen him be curious about her condi-tion, thoughtful about the information she'd relayed and most recently charming.

Now she was watching him at his most focused.

There would be yet another layer to him. When he had to confront Echo's men she would see the violence. While she understood why it was necessary, it wasn't something she was looking forward to. It would change him and she couldn't say how she would react to that change.

Then she shook her head. It didn't matter if her opinion changed or if he became less attractive to her. All of this was temporary. Their journey, Echo, the necklace…Tarak. Eventually it would be over and then she would return to her village and continue on with the life she'd created for herself.

Peaceful. Quiet. Studious. Helpful. It was her only option.

Unless Tarak was right. Unless she could find a way to control… No, she refused to accept it. If she'd been able to control the poison she would have certainly found a way by now. For over twenty years she'd lived like this. There was nothing in her past to suggest that she could live any other way.

Only because you never tried.

Lilith grimaced. There were times when listening to the inner truth of the mind was not very satisfying. Especially when she told herself that she couldn't believe what it was saying.

Rather than dwell on her thoughts she concentrated on the map Tarak was making in the dampening earth and the task in front of them.

"We're here. They're there." He pointed with the stick. "They'll probably only create a perimeter of about a hundred meters around the camp to patrol and her men will take shifts."

"How can you be certain?"

"It's what I would do if I were among them. The best we can do is eliminate one, and then hope another comes looking for his fallen mate. That will leave her with only one man back in camp. Once we have two on two I'll feel a little more confident in going after her on her turf."

Lilith nodded.

"You understand what's required?"

She lifted her gaze from the map and met his eyes. They were colder than she had ever seen them. It made her sad and it made her realize how she'd been able to forget at times who he was at his core.

A warrior. That's what the monks had called him. They were right.

"If it comes to it you're going to need to kill. Without remorse or hesitation. Both of our lives could depend on it."

"I understand."

Tarak shook his head. "No, I don't think you do, but we don't have time to waste. I need to be able to trust you, Lilly. Completely."

She took a deep breath and slowly let it out. "I understand. I will follow your orders. How will we get the necklace back from her?"

"Good question. But it's our last concern. First her men, then we worry about her. All right?"

"First her men. Then Echo," Lilith repeated. She felt the coldness she'd seen in his eyes settling in her own stomach. It was a sick feeling. She wondered how he lived with it. But she could also see how it helped. Cold quickly turned to numbness. Numb, she would be able to work in contrast to her beliefs in order to do what needed to be done.

"Tarak, please know that I do understand that if we have to kill her to get the necklace…then she dies."

Chapter 11

Allison Gracelyn carefully read the information being relayed to her by the information networks of Oracle. The computer hummed in the silent office of a now-empty town house in Alexandria, Virginia. Unable to sleep, she had chosen to work instead. Pushing herself and the resources available to her to their utmost capacity. And it had worked. She'd finally found what she was looking for.

She allowed a brief smile to cross her lips.

"Got you," she said.

South Africa.

India.

Allison had been tracking the messengers that Arachne had hired and deployed before her death for weeks. One messenger had succeeded in delivering his package to Kwan-Sook.

Through the now-dead crime boss, Allison had learned the dangerous fact that the data contained in the package was merely a portion of Arachne's information empire. So many world leaders' secrets out there somewhere in the world for anyone to find. Secrets that could be used to manipulate powerful figures for money, power, more information. It was a deadly cycle.

And knowing that what they had discovered and eventually lost was only a piece of the puzzle kept her awake at night, working.

But at least now, she knew where to find the other two packages.

South Africa.

India.

She leaned back in her leather chair and stretched. Long hours in front of a computer screen had tightened her muscles and the tension of knowing what was loose out there in the world hadn't helped.

"Who is there, Arachne?" she asked softly although she suspected she already knew the answer. "Your other daughters no doubt."

No, not daughters, Allison reminded herself. Biological offspring. There was a difference. Was it one of those offspring who had killed Kwan-Sook? Three daughters, each with a piece of a powerful empire. If they were anything like their biological mother in temperament it was only natural to assume that they wouldn't be satisfied with a mere piece of an empire.

Each one would want the whole enchilada. To get that they would need to destroy the others.

Or would they? What if nurture had won out over nature? What if these two women had been raised to know the difference between good and evil and the person who had stolen the information from Kwan-Sook was another figure entirely?

What if it turned out that Arachne's children were allies and not enemies?

If there was a chance of that, then there was a chance that Allison and the Oracle agents could track them down without complications. If these women offered no struggle, Allison could retrieve the data, destroy it and Arachne's legacy once and for all.

Maybe it was improbable, but even just the hope that the end was almost in sight was enough to have Allison thinking that she could take a few hours of sleep. She missed sleep.

In the end, whether these women were like Jackie or not wouldn't matter. Friend or foe the result would be the same. It had to be. The data—all of it—would be found and destroyed.

But if they were like Jackie…if they were out for the power that the data could bring them, Allison understood deeply what the cost of bringing down those two women might be. More lives could be lost.

Allison thought of Kwan-Sook, the giantess. Despite

her deformity she'd been a powerful enemy. What were the other two like? What genetic marvels had Jackie concocted in her secret lab?

There was only one way to find out.

South Africa.

India.

It was where she would start.

Chapter 12

"You know what to do?" Tarak whispered as close to Lilith's ear as he dared get.

Just before they had left their camp he'd smothered the fire. In the waning glow of the embers Lilith's skin practically glowed. There was no doubt that in her current state she was lethal.

"Stay covered. No matter what happens. Don't give them anything to shoot at."

She nodded, but he wouldn't know how she would react until the moment was upon them. They had been over the plan several times, but their preparation would mean nothing if Lilith froze at a crucial moment.

He thought back to how she had handled herself the night Echo torched her village. Standing tall in the midst of destruction and ultimately death. She had calmly looked into the eyes of a tiger and assured him it wouldn't attack, shooing it away like a kitten rather than a ferocious predator. No, she wouldn't freeze. He was all but sure of it.

Whether she knew it or not she was a natural soldier. Focused. Calm under pressure and determined when she needed to be.

In a way, that made him sad. What he was asking of her would change her. Tonight she would not use her powers solely for defense. Tonight he was asking her to attack. He couldn't be sorry for it given what was at risk, but he was willing to accept culpability in turning an innocent woman into a necessary weapon.

Choosing to wait until the deepest part of the night, Tarak hoped to use fatigue and the night against Echo and her men. It was now that hour. He'd lead them as close as possible to Echo's camp just outside the imaginary perimeter he concluded her men would protect. Now it was time to see if his predictions were right about the pattern her men would follow.

Twenty minutes later he heard the steady movement of someone walking through the jungle, obviously not concerned with making too much noise. Or maybe hopeful that any noise he did make would frighten off small animals.

It was definitely a predator. But a human one.

Listening carefully, Tarak shifted in his stance,

readying himself for action. As the footsteps got closer Tarak moaned.

"Help," he groaned. He waited another beat. "Please help."

The footsteps stopped. He'd been heard. He ruffled the bush in front of him just in case the man hadn't been able to determine where the sound had been coming from. There was another pause. No doubt the man was trying to decide what to do. Ultimately he would have to investigate. Tarak was sure of that. The question was whether or not he would shoot first and investigate later.

When Tarak heard the man make a step forward, then the sound of the gun being cocked, he acted. He jerked up from his hiding position,, his arms in the air. He pretended to fall to his side a bit to give the impression of weakness.

"Help me. I'm lost from my camping party. I think something bit my leg."

Tarak couldn't see the man's face, but he did notice that the gun was still pointed directly at his heart. A careful soldier, the man obviously believed in taking precautions.

"Are you with a rescue party?"

"Who the fuck are you?" was the low, guttural response.

Only there was no need to answer him. At that moment Lilith rolled down from the tree branch she'd been perched on directly over the spot where Echo's man stood. The spot they had picked out earlier as the best chance to get behind anyone who would come after Tarak. Her knees hooked around the branch, she was able to hang above the man like a bat without making a sound. She touched the side of his face and in seconds, before he could even consider what had touched him he was on the ground convulsing.

A few coughs and sputters. Then the convulsing stopped.

Lilith pulled herself up to the branch, held it for a second while she unhooked her knees and let herself somersault off the tree onto the ground.

She walked toward him and Tarak could see already the guilt in her. Even without being able to see her face.

"You didn't act according to the plan."

"But…I… He's dead."

"The cue was my first line. You were supposed to act after I said something bit my leg. You waited. It could have cost me my life. Don't do it again."

His words were harsh, but they had been used deliberately. Now she was focused on what could have gone wrong rather than what she did. And considering that his life might have been at risk would show her that she'd had no choice.

Or she would be pissed at him. Either way it would take her mind off the guilt.

"The next one should come along looking for his mate following the same perimeter. I don't know how long that will take, so you'll need to be patient. Let's move the body a little closer to their camp and we'll find another tree that works."

"You're certain the next man will come alone?" Lilith asked.

"Hard to know. We need to be prepared for two. At that point if I have to shoot one it's not as if we have to worry about compromising the element of surprise. Echo will figure out that we've come for her, but by that point she'll be outnumbered."

"We still need a way to get around her force field."

"Working on it," Tarak promised. "Help me drag the body."

Again she hesitated, glancing down at the man who only seconds ago had been alive.

"Now, Lilith. We have no time to waste."

His words seemed to snap her out of whatever thoughts she was dwelling on because she bent down and grabbed an arm.

Good soldier, he thought. Very good soldier.

Echo blinked open an eye. Something or someone had disturbed her sleep. As a rule she didn't like to have her sleep disturbed. It tended to make her grumpy.

She heard whispering beyond on the other side of the fire and was forced to open her other eye. That's when she sensed it. The small tickle at the back of her neck. The buzz in her ear. Her senses kicked into overdrive and she could feel that the protective perimeter of air around her had been penetrated. Movement inside. Something big. Moving closer. Definitely a threat.

She always knew when it was a threat.

Sitting up, she could see Rolf standing as he said something to Kent.

"What is it?"

"Burns hasn't come back from patrol. He's overdue. I was going to go look for him."

Echo sighed. "Don't bother. He's dead."

She watched Kent and Rolf stare at her over the fire with suspicion, doubt and a whole lot of fear in their faces. At least in Rolf's face. Kent showed nothing. "Someone's coming."

"Who?" Kent asked. He stood and immediately reached for the gun in his holster.

"Hmm…hard to tell," Echo allowed. "Could be an animal. Definitely an enemy. If Burns hasn't come back by now whatever is out there has him already."

"Burns knows what he's doing. He's good in a fight. He might not be dead," Rolf said.

Echo shook her head. "Moron. If he wasn't dead he'd be back. Or at the very least we would hear him shouting for help or hear gunfire. Do you hear anyone shouting? Do you hear gunfire?"

"No," Rolf conceded. "But I also don't know how you know that there is something out there. It's not like we set up trip wires."

Echo tapped her temple with her finger. "I have my own trip wires right up here. Trust me. We'll move out together. If it's an animal, three guns against it should do the trick. If it's not then whoever it is might not be expecting three of us."

Kent nodded his agreement and Rolf, bless him, would ultimately always do as she asked. Tonight was no exception.

When they got out of this jungle and back to civilization she was actually considering keeping him on as a pet. Usually, on jobs like this, she liked to dispose of the tools she worked with. It wasn't good for anyone in her organization to have too much information and the fact that Rolf and Kent knew that Lilith still existed was a liability.

But in Rolf's case his loyalty was outweighing his liability.

Kent, of course, would have to die. She'd already scripted his death in her head. She was going to love watching his shocked face the moment he knew he'd been double-crossed.

Of course, none of that would happen until she'd extracted all the usefulness out of him that she could.

"Let's go."

Lilith sat on the branch, her back against the trunk of the tree, and tried desperately to keep the image of the fallen man out of her mind. She told herself that she'd known what was expected of her and was simply following the plan, but that didn't work. She told herself that if she hadn't acted then he would have shot Tarak. And she believed it to be true. But that didn't work, either.

She had killed. Deliberately. The act was such a betrayal of everything she had ever been taught by the monks, she wondered if it might not fracture her spirit.

Do no harm. It was a relatively simple teaching. The very first precept. And one that in the past she had worked to forgive herself for breaking because she had no control over what she'd done. Now that was not the case.

And so she was changed. She was a woman of violence.

Lilith glanced down at the bush where she knew Tarak waited. She wanted to blame him for making her do what she'd done. It would be easy. He could have found a way to take down the man on his own without shooting him and giving away their location. He had a knife. He had his hands. He could have wrestled the man, broken his neck.

Maybe he'd wanted her to do it. Maybe he'd purposely set her up to kill so that he could turn her into a creature of violence just like him. The dark thoughts pelted her and she was at a loss to stop them.

He knew about the necklace. He thought he knew about how powerful the information inside it was. What if this was his way of turning her? First he makes her kill. Then again. Then when they have necklace back he convinces her to take the next step. To use the information to control people. To make money. To build an empire on the foundation of other people's lies, crimes and secrets. All the while telling her how much he wants her. Seducing her with words if not his body.

How could she know? How could she be certain it wasn't true?

When in doubt rely on your heart. Or your gut. Same thing in my opinion.

Lilith shook her head, startled at how clearly the

familiar words sounded in her mind. Sister Peter was forever telling Lilith that every good decision she'd ever made, every right one, she'd made by following her gut. The decision to leave medical school, to become a nun, to follow her path to India. Lilith used to tease her about her gut leading her all the way to a leper colony in India, but Sister Peter would smile and say it was the best decision she'd ever made. Her gut, her heart, had not steered her wrong. She believed it was there where her God resided.

Only, now she was dead.

Still, Lilith was pretty sure that if she could speak to Sister Peter, even after her death, she would claim that she had made the right choice. That she was at peace with her decision and the way she'd lived her life.

So what was in Lilith's gut?

She'd been drawn to Tarak from the start. Certainly she'd trusted him enough to help her on her mission even though she knew he was dangerous. Now she might go as far as to say that she was bound to him in some fundamental way. She'd slept near him. Shared a crude roof. She'd done that with no man since her father.

It had been nice. In spite of the frustration she'd felt in knowing she couldn't touch him. For the first time in a long time she hadn't felt alone.

Which didn't make sense.

From the moment she'd arrived in India she had never been alone. She'd been part of the community in the village. But she hadn't been a nun, or a villager or a monk. A part of the community yes, but not one of them.

And there it was. More than his charm, or his intensity or even his handsome face, Tarak didn't make her feel separate or different from others. They were alike on some level. That was what drew her to him. That was what was in her gut.

Perhaps it was that realization of how similar they were that made her want to doubt him. Despite the years of teachings and her wish to be a true Buddhist, ultimately she was more like Tarak than she was like the monks. More ready for action than she was for striving toward a higher spiritual plane.

She smiled sadly in the dark. Perhaps the next life. But apparently not in this one.

The dark thoughts that had plagued her receded. Again she glanced down to where she knew Tarak waited. Silently she apologized for doubting him. He was a man of violence, and she was capable of it, too, but together they would serve a greater good. She was sure of it.

A rustle of noise caught her attention and instantly her senses kicked into gear. She could feel her heart pounding as a rush of adrenaline filled her system. Glancing down at her uncovered hand, she could see nothing in the dark, but she wondered briefly if the tone of her skin had changed in the last few seconds. Inwardly she felt different. As if something that had been dormant had suddenly sprung to life.

Quickly she dismissed the foolish idea and prepared to execute phase two of the plan. Expecting another of Echo's men to come looking for their lost comrade, Tarak would once more use distraction to set up the kill for Lilith. Once they eliminated Echo's man they would move on to the camp and take out Echo's last man as they prepared to deal with her.

Lilith still wasn't sure how they would get around Echo's force field but she imagined they would face that when the time came. Echo could not escape them this night. Not if Lilith could do anything to stop her.

She was completely unprepared for the high-pitched laughter that rang out from the ground below.

"Well, look at what we have here," Echo called out. "Told you Burns was dead."

Lilith slowly lowered her eyes to see three people below, not one as they'd hoped, looking down at the body.

"What the hell happened to him?" the one Echo had called Rolf asked.

"Can't you see? Look at his face. It's poison."

"Snake bite?" the other man asked.

"Something like that," Echo muttered.

Lilith slowly turned back again, her gaze falling to the bush where Tarak was still hiding. Not so much as a leaf moved. Obviously he'd heard Echo's voice and knew that their plan wouldn't work. Not against three of them. The element of surprise was gone and with it their advantage.

She watched for some kind of signal but she knew

that even the slightest movement might reveal his position. His nonmovement was signal enough. Pressing back against the trunk, Lilith willed herself invisible.

"Interesting. First the fuel lines, now this. Looks like simple little Lilith isn't so simple after all. I knew it. I knew I had been had by that poor-village-girl act. That bitch!"

"What does that mean?" asked one of her men. Lilith wasn't sure which.

"Don't you get it? She's here. She followed us. Somehow. Come out, come out wherever you are!"

Lilith closed her eyes and stilled her breathing.

"I know you're out there," Echo tried again. "Another special gift of mine. I can sense when something dangerous has entered, well…let's just call it my personal space. Why don't you show yourself so we can end this once and for all?"

Lilith continued to remain still, even as the three of them began spreading out to check the area around the body, rustling some of the larger rhododendron bushes that could shelter a person.

"Even if it was your sister who did this…"

"Don't call her that!" Echo spat.

"Whatever. Even if she did this she could have already left the area."

"She hasn't," she assured the taller of the two men. Lilith opened her eyes to thin slits and saw that Echo was directly below her. If she jumped now would Echo be able to erect her force field before Lilith could lay a hand on her? Certainly her men would shoot her, but at least Echo would be dead. Her only thought was of Tarak. What would happen to him?

She wasn't concerned with her own life. She'd already accepted that it would be worth any sacrifice to stop Echo from leaving the country with the necklace. But it wasn't fair to sacrifice him, as well. Tarak shouldn't have to pay for what Lilith's mother had been. For what Echo was.

"She won't leave until she has this."

Lilith watched as Echo reached into the V of her T-shirt and pulled out the large gold spider necklace.

"This is what you want, isn't it?" she shouted. "Come take it, if you're brave enough."

No, Lilith thought. Echo was too prepared for the attack. If there was a way around her force field Lilith had to believe it would be easier to find it when Echo was not expecting her. She watched as Echo removed a gun from a holster under her arm and began firing randomly in different directions, including the direction of Tarak's hiding spot.

A wild keening sound filled the air as soon as the report of the bullets faded.

"That's a big cat. Maybe a leopard."

"Scared, Kent?" Echo asked. "Of a kitty cat?"

"You might be more scared if you didn't have that shield that you can just throw up to protect yourself. Look, what the hell are we doing? We can't see shit. It's the middle of the night. I say we head back to camp and wait until dawn. Then we cross the river and get the hell out of here. If someone's chasing us then we outrun them, as simple as that."

There was silence for a moment.

"Kent's right, Echo. We can't fight something we can't see. And if it is the girl—well, she's not the only poisonous thing out here. You have the necklace. She can't get it back. Let's stay focused."

"Cowards. I'm surrounded by cowards. Did you hear that, Lilith? I'm leaving now. If you want Mummy's necklace back you're going to have to show yourself."

There would be time, Lilith told herself. They were still at least a day's hike from civilization. More than enough time to catch up with Echo and wait for the right time to act. Sacrifice was one thing, but only if it accomplished her goal. Echo was too alert. There would be a better time. There had to be.

"Fine." Echo pushed the necklace back inside her shirt. "Stay in your hidey-hole, but know that I'll be watching my back. I knew I should have killed you when I had the chance. I should have shot you the second I got off the damn helicopter."

No, Lilith told herself. *I should have killed you.*

Chapter 13

She waited eighteen minutes. Lilith knew because she had counted every second in her head. Her eyes remained locked on the bush below where Tarak still had not moved. As each second ticked by she thought about the shots that Echo had fired from her gun. She thought about how some had been in the direction of Tarak.

One reason she remained still on her branch was simply that she didn't want to go down there and find him dead. She didn't want to be responsible for another life. She didn't want to be alone in the jungle with no one to help her stop a madwoman.

But most of all she didn't want him to be dead because…she didn't.

At eighteen minutes and four seconds, the branches

started to rustle and she could see him extract himself from where he'd been hiding. So quietly, so smoothly had she not had her eyes glued to the spot she wouldn't have seen him emerge.

"Lilly."

The quiet call from below jolted her into action. With a fluidity of motion, she reached out for a nearby branch and let her weight drop as she swung down to the ground a foot away from him.

"Do we go after them?" she asked.

"What did she mean when she said another special gift? That garbage about the air around her personal space."

"I do not know. It was as if she could feel us somehow. Sense that we were close. Part of her skills along with the force field."

Tarak rubbed his eyes with one hand. "You certainly don't come from the most normal family in the world, do you? All right. We now have to assume that she can tell when we're getting close. You heard what they said?"

Lilith nodded. "They want to outrun us."

"Which means we have to stay close but not too close. We'll move out before dawn and do our best to stay on their trail."

"And then what?"

Lilith couldn't see much in the pitch-dark of night but she could tell by his stillness that her question annoyed him.

"Then we… Yeah. Still haven't figured that one out

yet. And now it's more complicated. How the hell do we steal something from someone who can tell when we're close and can put up a shield against any attack?"

Certain the question wasn't directed at her, Lilith turned away to look for a place where they could sit tight for the next few hours. Next to the tree seemed the best bet. Not that she was worried about predators sneaking up on them. She had no plans to sleep for the rest of the night.

"I cannot keep asking you to do this," she finally confessed even though she couldn't imagine what she would do without him. "This is my responsibility. I have to get the necklace back and destroy what's inside it. You've already done enough. You've led me to her. I…I can go on from here. On my own."

And the next time, if she was faced with the decision of offering her life to stop Echo, she could do it knowing that Tarak would be safe. That she wasn't risking him in the process.

Tarak let out a sound that might have been a huff. Then he crouched down to a squat so that he was eye level with her. "Really? What would you do next?"

"Follow her. Wait for a chance to act. Maybe try to confront her again."

"Ah, confrontation. Let's see. The first time you tried it, she killed your friend. Just now when you had the chance you didn't move. She was right below you. You must have seen her."

"I could not be sure you would be safe."

"No. You could not be sure you could accomplish what you needed to do and get out alive."

Was that true? In her heart was she not prepared to forfeit her life to stop Echo? It made her feel weak. "I must do anything," she whispered. "Everything. She is evil."

"She is. And I have no doubt that you will do what you need to do when the time comes. But admit it, Lilly. You're a practical little thing. A soldier at heart, you're on a mission. That mission has multiple parts. Retrieve the necklace, stop Echo and get out alive if you can. You know that your only chance to succeed with all three phases is to have help. My help. We're in this together. To the end."

"You just said you do not know what to do," she pointed out. "What if the end is also the end of your life? Sitting up in that tree, waiting, not knowing if you were alive or dead...I..."

"What?"

"I have never felt such panic. I did not like it. I do not want to feel it again."

"No, it's not a good feeling. But when you saw that I was alive how did you feel then?"

"Relieved," she admitted. "Happy. Maybe even euphoric."

"See," he said, smiling. She knew because she could see his gleaming white teeth against the blackness that surrounded them. "There is always balance."

"But we still do not know how to get the necklace,"

Lilith repeated, irritated that she could not think of a solution to the problem.

"I've got a few hours, haven't I?"

"I did not mean to criticize. I have no answers, either. I find this so frustrating. Wanting something that I am unable to obtain. In the village I had everything I needed. I was thirsty, I drank. I was hungry, I ate. I wanted knowledge and I studied. This is so different."

She heard a small chuckle and wondered what she said to make him laugh.

"Frustrating doesn't begin to cover it." Tarak stood and stepped back a few paces toward the dense thicket where she knew he'd left his gear. He returned with the backpack and sat close again, offering her his canteen.

"I should not. You cannot touch where I have put my lips. There could be drops of water left on the rim." Maintaining her water supply hadn't been a problem during their trek. Either she'd found a stream or had been lucky enough to find a few large leafs filled with rainwater for her to fill her water sack. But she knew it was dry. So did Tarak.

"I'll drink first, then you'll finish it. You need to be fresh for whatever happens tomorrow."

She saw the motion of him lifting the canteen to his mouth and tipping it back, then listened as he gulped heavily.

When he handed it to her again she thought about where her lips would go. She hesitated, realizing for the first time she would taste the essence of a man.

"It's all right. Just reach for the edge of the canteen. You won't touch me."

Without realizing it she almost had taken the canteen from his hand without her gloves. She'd removed them for the attack. She might have been able to blame the night's excitement on her carelessness if only she knew it wasn't true. Her carelessness had come from her eagerness to put the canteen to her mouth.

For a taste, she might have killed him.

Distressed, she put her hands behind her back. "No. Give me my gloves first. I must have them."

"I bet you don't need them now," Tarak countered. "I bet if you could see your hands you would see that the sheen has receded. They're gone. We're relatively safe here for a while. There would be no need for the poison to surface."

"My gloves."

Thankfully he didn't argue further. Instead he reached into one of the pockets on the backpack and pulled out the gloves. "Why can I touch these?"

Lilith felt the material fall into her lap. "The poison doesn't transfer. I wear silk to protect others because it's a tight weave. Not very porous. In case I touched someone the toxin would not pass through the material."

"I see. So I could touch you as long as you were clothed."

"Covered, yes."

"Covered," he repeated softly. "So as long as your body was covered in silk I might be able to touch your hand."

"Yes."

"Or your arm. Or your thigh. Or your belly."

Lilith shook her head. "No, you couldn't."

"I could. You said. I could touch you. Stroke you. Your breast. Your back. I might touch all of that as long as it was draped in silk?"

Her breathing became shallow and her heart bumped against her chest. She felt flushed but it was different from when they had been waiting for Echo's men. This physical reaction was…pleasant. Almost.

"Why do your words make me feel this way?"

"Because you can imagine it. You can think about what it might be like for me to touch you and you can see in your mind that it would feel good."

"Does it?" Lilith pushed, desperately curious to know. "I have never been touched. Like in the way you are saying. What does it feel like?"

"Put your gloves on," Tarak commanded softly.

Lilith took one of the gloves from her lap and fitted her fingers inside it. Then she pulled until the material nearly reached her elbow. She repeated the same process with the other one. When she was done she sensed a fraction of movement and then before she could pull back Tarak had caught her around the wrists.

"Trust me. Close your eyes."

It wasn't as if she had a choice to trust him or not. Her trust was instinctive at this point.

Lilith closed her eyes on his suggestion and then waited in high anticipation for what was to come. He loosened his grip on her wrists. Then he slid his hands down until they were touching palm over palm. For a moment he didn't move and that sensation alone was fascinating. The warmth and weight of his hands on top of hers.

He took her right arm in his and ran one strong hand up her arm to the point where the material ended, turning it slightly on the journey back down, then up again and down. The sensation was hypnotic. She felt like a cat being petted and suddenly understood why they purred.

Switching hands, he repeated the slow, even movements, this time turning her hand up and rubbing slow circles on the place where her wrist met her palm. Her pulse jumped and Lilith wondered if he could feel the change in the beat where his thumb rested.

His fingers touched the tips and waited there for a breath. It was the slightest connection between them and yet it felt as if they were inseparable. Finally he linked his fingers between hers, gently moving his hand so that she could feel them sliding together. Interlocking.

Her breath hitched and he tightened his grasp, connecting them in a way she'd never been to another human. This was what it meant to hold. To be held in return.

She opened her eyes and saw that he was staring down at their linked hands. His expression was indiscernible in the dark.

"It does feel good."

"Yes," he answered.

"It's like being part of someone. Not being just yourself. Does that make any sense?"

She could see in the moonlight another hint of white that signaled a smile. "Yes, it does. But you should know that it's not always like this. Sometimes touching doesn't feel like anything at all."

"How could that be?"

"I don't know. For some it's different. More important. For others it means nothing. When it does happen between two people they call it chemistry."

"We have chemistry," she confirmed. "Why do you think that is?"

"Because I must have really pissed off someone in a former life," he mused. "That or Buddha has a very sick sense of humor."

"I do not understand."

"It's ironic, that's all. That we should have this very strong chemistry, but can't take it any further."

Lilith tugged her hands back and felt his fingers slip from hers. The feeling of loss was instant. Perturbed, she wanted to blame him for even showing her such a thing existed, but she could not regret the experience.

"We should rest," she said as she found a nearly comfortable spot against the tree.

"For an hour or so, yes."

"You will come up with a plan." She felt confident that he would eventually.

"That's the idea. I suppose we'll just follow them. Wait for some kind of opening. Her radar or whatever the hell it is she's using to track us will let her know that we're following her. I wonder if it works as well if we're ahead of her. If we could get in front of them maybe we could find a way to separate her from her men. After that, who knows?"

"She cannot be unstoppable. If that were so then she would not have needed our mother's information to build her empire. She would already have one."

"Good point."

Satisfied with his agreement, Lilith tilted her head back against the tree and closed her eyes although she knew sleep would not come. She felt Tarak shift and move so that he, too, rested his back against the other side of the tree. They were back to back with the width of the tree between them and still she could feel his hand in hers. Could still hear in her head the sound of his breath quickening when their fingers linked.

"You have had…chemistry…with a woman before," Lilith stated although she wasn't sure why it mattered. She was not completely ignorant of the ways between men and women. She knew from the men in the village that their sexual drive could be very strong. For that matter the same could be said of the women. And it wasn't as if the monks and the nuns were without these feelings. It was what made their celibacy a sacrifice. Still the idea of Tarak touching another filled her with a burst of anger. No, not anger. Envy. A destructive feeling she'd worked hard to eliminate in herself. Clearly she had not succeeded.

"I have. But of all the things I've done with a woman I've never spent the night holding someone's hand. Reach back."

Lilith considered what he was offering. In reality it could be dangerous. She knew that contact with her gloved hand would not kill directly, but over time, if the toxin should absorb through...

The poison is gone for now.

It was a fleeting thought. One that Tarak had planted when he suggested she could have control over her power. But some latent instinct shouted to her that it was the truth. It was safe to touch him like this.

Reaching her arm back around the tree, she searched for and found his outstretched hand. She didn't think it strange, either, that she knew which hand would be waiting for her. Their fingers locked and rested on the ground.

Lilith took a deep breath and thought that maybe a quick nap would be all right. As long as Tarak was there with her.

Holding her hand.

Tarak blinked open his eyes. His training had allowed him a brief rest while still being in tune with his surroundings. Between the natural predators and the human ones, the consequences of letting down his guard could be fatal for both of them.

A glance up at the sky told him that a little more than an hour had passed. The darkness was softening. In another hour or so the sun would begin to rise. A tingle in his shoulder had him twisting a bit and he could feel Lilith's hand fall away from his. He shook the still-sleeping limb a few times and then quietly rolled to his feet.

He let his ears and his instincts do the searching for danger. He decided that if there was anyone nearby waiting to attack them they were better at the game than he was.

And he knew there were few that were.

He circled the tree they'd used for shelter and camouflage and crouched down to where Lilith still remained sleeping. Her head tilted ever so slightly to the right. Her lips were curved gently as if she smiled in her sleep.

Curious, he reached for his knapsack nearby and pulled out a smaller penlight designed to illuminate a specific target without giving away a position.

He flicked it on and aimed the light at her cheek. So perfectly smooth. Brown like heated caramel. She was perfection. If it weren't for the fact that she was deadly.

In repose there was no sheen on her skin, as he suspected. There was no reason to be alarmed, at least in this instant. He wondered if she believed him when he said she could control it. That there could be times in her life where she would not hurt the ones she touched.

He doubted it. The woman had gone her whole life and had never allowed herself to be touched. Never experimented once. Not that he could blame her. Apparently anytime anyone did reach for her it was violently and it immediately resulted in death.

Hell of lesson for a child to learn.

Maybe it was time for a new one.

Since caution had never been his strong point Tarak didn't think overly long about what he was about to do. He simply lifted his hand and with the stroke of his finger gently touched her cheek. One swish from the top of her cheekbone to the bottom of her chin.

Then he waited. And waited.

Nothing. No convulsions. No swelling in his finger or arm. No tightening in his chest. None of the usual symptoms of exposure to a nerve toxin. The man she'd touched only hours ago had gone down in seconds.

Happy to be right, he couldn't help but hum slightly under his breath. "Oh, the possibilities."

Lilith blinked open her eyes and he could see she was stunned to find him so close.

"Get back!" Instantly she scrambled away from him, trying to work her way around the tree and farther out of his reach. When he pointed the penlight at her face again he could literally see the shimmering essence that signaled the toxin seeping out of her skin.

"What were you doing?" she shouted at him, although still smart enough to do so in hushed tone so as not to alert anyone who might be listening. Good girl, Lilly. "I could have moved unexpectedly. I could have touched you!"

"I've got news for you, Lilly. I touched you."

She was standing now and checked her gloves furiously to see if they could have fallen off her hands. "Impossible."

"Actually, no. Right there on your cheek." He pointed to the spot. "Not the most scientific experiment in the world I'll grant you, but it proved that I was right. You're not as deadly as you think you are."

"That cannot be," she said, obviously mystified by his statement. "I have always been dangerous."

"Oh, darling. I didn't say anything about you not being dangerous. At the very least you're treacherous to my peace of mind. Come along. We'll talk while we walk. I think I might have a plan."

"You touched me knowing you could have died. I am thinking your next plan should be a little more sensible."

He might have been irritated by her lack of faith if he didn't find her absolutely charming when she was miffed.

As they headed out, Lilith fell back a few steps. She kept him in sight but the small distance between them allowed her the space she needed to think. To process what had happened.

He'd touched her, but he did not die.

Curious, she pulled off her glove and ran her hand over her cheek. She felt nothing but skin. No mark or indicator of where he'd touched her. No residue of feeling. She was furious with him for taking such a risk. But she was even more furious that he'd done it while she was asleep.

For the first time in her life she'd been touched and she didn't have the memory of it to take with her if she should die.

Chapter 14

"I can hear the water." Lilith stopped to listen to the sound. The rumble of fast rapids drowned out any noises from the jungle behind them.

"We're not far back," Tarak told her as he checked his GPS receiver once more.

"Do you think we can get in front of her like you said? Maybe set a trap?"

"Maybe. Whatever we plan we need to act soon. We're not far from where she should be able to find some transportation. If we can't stop her out here then trying to do so in New Delhi where she'll have more resources will be next to impossible."

Lilith thought about that. "Not if we have more resources, too."

He glanced over his shoulder at her with a raised eyebrow but she was unsure whether he was impressed with her suggestion or amused by her comment. After all, she certainly had no resources to call upon. Her world had been the village and the monastery.

But he came from a different world.

"Resources," he repeated.

"You must know people. People of violence rarely work alone. Like Echo's men. They come in packs."

"Okay, don't compare me to her thugs. They're all brawn and no brains. And most of them have ended up dead. I've been doing what I do for a very long time and as you can see I'm very much alive."

Lilith tried to stifle a snort but failed. She couldn't remember the last time she made such a sound. "Maybe you do not have as much brains as you think. You could have very easily been dead an hour ago. You had no idea that your theory would prove true."

"You don't live life like I do without taking chances and relying on your gut instinct. I knew when I touched you I wasn't going to die. And I was right. You need to understand, Lilly, people like me, we're a breed apart. For the most part the world is grateful we exist."

"We… So there are more of you?"

"There are. There were. Good men. Good fighters all of them," Tarak said, his face tightening.

"Something happened."

"I lost several men on a mission in South America.

It's how I ended up with a bullet in my leg and empti-
ness in my soul."

"You were to blame?"

He laughed softly. "No, but it doesn't matter, does it?
I can't *not* feel the guilt. I hired them. I took them to that
place and they died. It doesn't really matter how."

"Like with Sister Peter."

"Exactly. You didn't cause her death, but you feel it.
Inside. That's how it was with my men. I used some CIA
contacts to set up that mission. One of them was a
friend. I hope the other was the traitor."

"If you contacted this friend would he come?"

"She might, yes. She always loved a grand adventure.
If it comes down to it we can reach her once we get to
Bomdila. If she'll agree to meet us with her team we
may have a better chance against Echo."

"That is if we do not catch up with Echo here. Now."

Tarak pushed through a heavy thicket and suddenly
the roar of the water was intense. Waves of white foam
flew over rocks at incredible speed. Lilith thought of the
heavy rains they had trekked through. Of course the
river was swollen. A small tributary, this river would
eventually flow into the Brahmaputra, but for all its
speed and force it could have been the mighty river.

Suddenly Tarak's arm was against her stomach forcing her back among the bushes.

"You must stop touching me," she insisted as she
backed away from the pressure of his forearm against
her midriff.

"Shh. Look out there. About a hundred and fifty meters down river. It's them trying to cross."

Lilith ducked behind Tarak, but, following his finger, she could see through the bushes to the threesome attempting to navigate the river by foot. Where they crossed Lilith could see boulders and rocks poking out over the water peaks. It would be a difficult crossing, but with balance and a little luck they would make it to the other side.

Balance, luck and time.

"This could be our shot. It's going to take them a while to get across. The river is narrow up here. It's rough, but we should be able to walk along the bottom of it. If we can make it to the other side before them then we'll have our chance to move ahead."

But Lilith shook her head. "I cannot."

"You can't swim?"

"No, the water will be freezing. Runoff from the mountains."

Tarak scowled. "If this is about being a little cold…"

"You do not understand. The cold water makes me sick. My pores close and the poison backs up. It makes me sick."

"Control the poison," Tarak ordered.

Inexplicably hurt, Lilith shook her head. "You ask me to control the beating of my heart. I cannot."

"You can."

Lilith searched for another answer and found it. Up river from where Echo was crossing there was a simple rope bridge. A base rope to walk across and two others to hold for balance.

"They must not have seen it," she said even as she pointed to it.

"Or they didn't want to take the time to go out of their way only to find that the damn thing would be unstable," Tarak grumbled. "Look at it. We're talking three ropes. Who knows what kind of condition it's in?"

"We're close enough to Bomdila that there would be camping and water rafting in these parts. A bridge like that is used by guides to get tourists across the river. It will hold us." Lilith was almost sure of it.

Tarak ran a hand over his chin. "Once we get out there we'll be exposed."

"They will be too concerned with getting over the rocks. Quickly. If we do not move now we may lose our advantage."

Lilith took the decision out of his hands and followed the shoreline for several meters until she reached the crude bridge. She turned to see if Tarak was behind her and was startled to find him so close. It was hard to believe that only a little more than a week ago he'd had a bullet in his leg.

It was a testament to his strength and a reminder that this was not a man to be taken lightly. Not that she believed she ever had.

Tarak turned his attention to the bridge and the water. He found the trees that served as the anchor for the ropes and tested to see how securely they were fastened. He tugged with all his strength but they remained tight.

"Well?"

"The ropes appear to be in good condition," he admitted. Then his gaze drifted out over the rushing rapids. "It's higher up than I realized. At least a five-foot drop. With the rushing water, if you fall you'll be carried away so fast there will be no way to stop you. And that's not considering what might break once you hit the rocks."

"Then I must not fall."

Tarak glared at her. "I don't like this."

"We do not have a choice. If we wait until they cross and try to follow their path we will still be that much farther behind. If we cross now and start running we can get ahead of them. I know we can. Please. We have to act now."

"Fine," he relented. "I'll go first. You stay behind me. And stay low."

Tarak ducked under the support rope and stepped onto the lead rope. Lilith could see how he adjusted his feet on the thick rope to balance his weight. He paused for a second, glancing over his shoulder at his backpack, but he must have decided it was worth the effort to carry it across because he carefully placed one foot in front of the other and began to move out over the river.

Lilith quickly followed although allowing some space between them in case she lost her balance. She didn't want Tarak to be the first thing she reached for. Her gloves made gripping the rope on either side of her waist more challenging, but she'd often had to walk tightrope bridges such as these. They were used among the people of her village as pathways over waterways.

Of course, she'd never attempted to use a bridge like this over such fast rushing water while chasing three people who were armed.

But Lilith imagined there was a first time for everything.

Step by step Tarak moved out over the rapids. The roaring sound below made any attempt at conversation pointless. Lilith followed, copying his style of one foot in front of the other while her knees were bent as much as she could to shrink her height.

Her last thought before she heard the crack of the gun was that they were almost halfway there.

"Watch the rock to your left up ahead. It's slippery."

Echo saw Rolf's mouth moving as he tried to tell her something, but she couldn't hear a thing. The idiot. What made him think that anyone could hear anything except the sound of water....

A tickle at the back of her neck ran all the way down to the base of her spine. So strong she had to work to maintain her balance on the rock bridge that barely broke the surface of the water. Her combat boots gave her the traction she needed and after a second's hesitation to secure her position, she allowed her senses to open.

Someone was close. Her head swirled to her left and then to her right. It took her a second to process what she was seeing. Far enough away that it was difficult to make out the figures, but her senses weren't lying. Over the water. Two people. A rope bridge.

The bridge that she'd dismissed using because she didn't want to lose time going backward. It was one of her faults. She tended to be impatient. Besides, there were enough rocks for her to cross where they were. If Kent and Rolf struggled that was their problem, but she had no intention of slowing down.

Her eyes narrowed. It was easy to make out that the first person on the bridge was a man. Dark hair. Dark skinned. Most likely a native. Carrying a pack on his back. He might have been a guide. A tourist out seeking adventure in the jungle.

But behind him was a woman. The gloves gave her away.

Interesting. Lilith had a friend.

That's how she'd managed to track them through the jungle. Echo smiled. She'd been giving Lilith far too much credit. Obviously it was with the help of the man that she'd managed to get so close and had been able to take out one of Echo's team. Lilith was as pathetic as Echo had originally suspected, needing a man's help.

Echo looked at the two men in front of her. Each were slowly navigating from one rock to the next, carefully choosing their steps and waiting a second between each before taking another. Yes, she had a team with her, but they were completely superfluous. More for show than anything else. Disposable. Replaceable.

Definitely unnecessary.

Echo removed a gun from her holster. She could shoot them both now and it wouldn't slow her down for a second. She could shoot them, shoot the man on the bridge and then it would just be her and Lilith.

Briefly Echo considered what Mummy would think of her two little girls battling it out. Then she remembered that there had been a reason why each of the sisters had been given a piece of the empire. A piece that wasn't nearly as valuable without the other two. Each one got a taste of what was at stake. A way to tease the palate. It was only natural that each would want more. Or it should have been natural.

Obviously Lilith was unnatural in that regard. Because despite Lilith's valiant efforts to follow Echo, she was fairly certain it wasn't to get the information back so Lilith could use it herself. No, there was a streak of altruism in her little sister that was as shiny as the gold necklace hanging around Echo's neck.

Good old Mummy had set it up so that the strongest would prevail and take from the others what was rightfully hers. Kwan-Sook had been no more than a blip on Echo's radar. Lilith should have been less so only here she was still coming after Echo like a pit bull with a rope between its teeth.

Echo glanced at her men. Rolf had made it to land. Kent wasn't far behind. No, she didn't need them, but at this point there was no reason to waste the bullets. Instead she aimed out to where the man was suspended over the river just beyond the halfway point.

"You want to come after me, sister, you do it alone." Echo narrowed her eyes, focused on the target and pulled the trigger.

Lilith saw Tarak buckle before the sound of the crack registered in her brain. She watched blood spit out of his shoulder and then, after some jerky flailing, he lost his balance and started to fall.

Miraculously he managed to catch himself with his other hand by holding on to one of the balance ropes even as his legs dangled over the water. He tried to swing his body forward and reach for the lead rope with his leg but missed.

Lilith took a step forward and then stopped. "Tarak," she called, although her voice was so breathy she knew he couldn't hear her. All she could do was watch as he struggled to use his other hand to reach for the rope but his bloodied shoulder wouldn't cooperate.

"Lilly, you need to take my hand and pull me up so I can get a leg over the bottom rope."

Lilith reached down and offered her hand. It wasn't far enough. She could see the struggle in his face as he tried to lift his shoulder. Crouching down on her two feet that were clinging to the single rope, she reached out even farther. He managed to swing his arm so that for a brief second she caught his hand. But it quickly slipped off the silken material of her glove.

"You need to take the glove off, Lilly. I need to catch you and hold your hand for leverage."

"I cannot. It will kill you."

"No, it won't. You know I'm not your enemy. There is no need to have your defenses up. Take a deep breath and feel yourself take control of the poison."

"It is impossible."

"Lilly! Now. I can't hold this rope much longer."

"I could try to reach for your leg." Even as she said it she tried to crouch even lower to reach down for his leg, but then she felt her balance wavering.

"You can't without falling. Just take the damn glove off and reach for my hand. You won't kill me if you touch me, I promise. I can't say the same if I fall. Hurry."

Lilith saw him grimace as a wave of pain crossed over him. The muscles in the arm holding on to the rope were strained and bulging, but as strong as he was he couldn't lift his body weight with only one arm. His grip was tight but she could see that his knuckles were blanched white. He would only be able to hold on for so long.

She looked at the water below and tried to see if maybe falling wasn't his better option. The current would take him down river, but if he could find a rock or a branch to grab hold of he might… The thought was instantly crushed by the image of what might happen if his body slammed into one of those rocks.

It was true. She was his best option.

"I…I will not kill you," she said aloud. She needed to hear the words. Needed to believe them. She began to pull the glove off her hand. She let it fall and watched as it was sucked up by the rushing water below.

Looking down at herself, she found it almost strange to see her bare hand. It wasn't often that it was uncovered, and in a strange daze she noted that her nails had grown too long.

"I will not kill you. I will not kill you."

"Now feel yourself taking control," Tarak shouted to her over the rushing water. "There are no enemies on this bridge. Just you and me. You can do this, Lilly. I need for you to do this."

He'd spoken of a sheen that covered her skin, the glimmering quality that signaled the poison. Looking at her hand now, she could see no evidence of it. Closing her eyes, she breathed in deep and willed herself to believe that she had control over her body. She could feel her heart beat heavily. Could feel the blood rushing through her system. Visualizing herself as a normal woman who was incapable of killing a man she cared about, she reached out as Tarak swung his arm forward at the same time.

She caught his hand in hers. Linked her fingers between his. And pulled him toward the rope. She waited for the convulsions but none came. Instead he was cursing under his breath and working to maintain his grip.

It was the first time she'd ever touched anyone who hadn't died. She wanted to sob because the emotions were so powerful, but there was no time.

Finally Tarak gripped the rope with his wounded

arm. Shouting in agony, he still managed to pull himself up so that his feet were on the bottom rope. Once he had his balance he could duck under the lead rope and begin making his way to the other side.

Lilith followed as fast as her feet would take her. Both of them crouched low. Both of them waiting for the report of another gunshot.

"Damn it." Echo hadn't hit the bastard hard enough. She raised the gun to fire again, but a wave rushed up over her ankles, then another as high as her knees. She struggled to maintain her stability on the rocks.

"Let's go!"

She glanced up at Rolf, who was waving her on, obviously concerned with the speed and swell of the waves. She looked again to her target and saw that they were almost on the other side of the river. Overhanging trees obscured her line of vision. It wasn't worth it to waste the bullet. Her only consolation was that at least he was wounded.

If nothing else that would slow them down.

"All right. I'm coming. Keep your panties on, boys." With a few more careful steps she ignored Rolf's out-stretched hand and instead took one last leap. Her boots met solid ground.

"Let's move," she ordered. "Fast. I want out of this damn jungle."

"You think she'll still follow us?" Kent had obviously seen what happened on the bridge.

Echo frowned. "You know, I think she's stupid enough to do just that. Even alone. I'm really going to have to come up with a suitable way to kill her if the fool actually manages to find me."

Chapter 15

"Ahhhh!!!!"

"It hurts very much, then?" Lilith tugged her bottom lip between her teeth out of concern. She'd never felt so ineffectual in her life.

"Yes," he said tightly. "Very much."

They were sitting on the bank of the river tucked behind some bushes to obscure their position, not that Lilith imagined Echo would be looking for them. She'd already done enough damage.

Tarak held his hand over the wound but Lilith could see the blood oozing out between his fingers.

"My pack," he said between clenched teeth. "I have a first-aid kit."

Losing the pack had been the first thing she'd told

him to do once they made it to land, hoping that the loss of the extra weight might relieve the pain in his shoulder. More difficult was sliding off the gun holster. Tarak had complied with both orders, but he didn't seem to be hurting any less.

Lilith rummaged through the knapsack and found a sealed watertight bag filled with gauze, medical tape and antiseptic. Plus a needle and a thread.

"Am I going to have to remove the bullet?" She'd seen it done once by Sister Peter but had never participated in the surgery herself. Her only job had been to stop the pain.

"It feels like it passed through. Check my back. Tell me what you see."

She scooted around behind him and saw a tear through his shirt that was a pretty good indicator that the bullet had passed completely through his flesh. Carefully, using her gloved hand despite knowing that her direct touch wouldn't kill him, she lifted the shirt high along his back almost to his neck and found a jagged hole about the size of a penny oozing blood.

"What should I do?"

"Use the antiseptic and try to clean it first. Then tape it up. Does it look like it might need stitching?"

"No." At the most one or two stitches might have helped to pull the skin together, but she imagined the gauze would suffice. Having witnessed a number of amputations the sight of blood shouldn't have affected her, but knowing that it was Tarak's blood made it different. His suffering touched her and made her hurt inside. Applying the antiseptic was only going to make it worse.

He'd been right about being able to control her condition to help pull him back onto the bridge. Could she control it enough to give him the right dosage that would take away his pain without completely immobilizing him?

Always when she anesthetized someone there had been risk. Had she diluted the toxin enough or too much? There was never any sense of certainty or confidence that the person taking her particular brand of medicine would eventually recover from it.

But if she could control not just the on or off trigger but the levels of poison in her skin, she might be able to offer something truly useful to people. A way to end pain without wondering if she would also end a life.

Even as the thoughts intruded she could see the back of her hand shimmer and glow. The temptation to lay her hand on his back, to stop his agony was almost overwhelming. What had he called it? A *gut feeling?* That's what she had now. An inner sense that if she touched him it would be all right.

Common sense, however, overruled her gut. Here in the middle of the jungle was not the time to be experimenting with her curse.

No. Not curse. Gift. At least maybe someday.

Instead she concentrated on retracting the poison and as she did the shimmer began to fade. The rush of what she could do was almost enough to make her forget that Tarak's wound was still bleeding.

"Don't worry about me. Just pour the damnable stuff on and be done with it."

Lilith pushed his shirt up and over his neck, carefully removing it to avoid any extra jostling. Then she took the antiseptic packets and tore them open. As soon as the liquid hit the wound she heard him hiss and knew that the small, whispery sound was only a fraction of what he was actually feeling.

The wound bubbled for a time, sucking out the bits of dirt and pieces of cotton from his shirt, and then Lilith patched him up. She repeated the process on the entry wound right at the spot where his arm met his shoulder. "You were lucky. The bullet missed bone and went through nothing but muscle and fat."

"Fat? Excuse me?"

Lilith glanced up from her work were she was taping down the padding over the wound.

"I think you mean muscle only."

Confused, Lilith shook her head. "No, I meant the fat under your arm. Are you sensitive about this?"

"Don't be ridiculous. Men aren't sensitive about fat. Still, what you are referring to is in fact muscle."

Since his face was unnaturally pale Lilith decided not to press the issue.

"We're going to lose them." He sighed.

"I know. Lie back. Rest your head on your pack."

"Are you disappointed? Angry maybe?" he asked

before the groaning replaced any coherent words as she helped him to recline.

The question startled Lilith. "Angry? It was my decision to use the bridge. Mine to even bring you along. All of this is my fault. It is you who should be angry with me."

"Furious," he teased.

"Besides that you have given me possibly the greatest gift anyone has ever given another person. I am not angry. I am so joyful I cannot even properly comprehend it."

He held her gaze and slowly smiled. "I am glad."

She smiled back and felt the tension in her cheeks. Smiling was such a rare occurrence for her, but she enjoyed the sensation of it. "Of course, we are still going to need to find a way to stop Echo."

His smile only widened. "Of course."

"Hello! Hello! Is anyone out there?"

Lilith pulled away from Tarak at the sound of the strange voices coming from the jungle.

"Oh my gosh, Bob, was that a gunshot? Is somebody shooting?" said an English-speaking woman with an American accent. "Boys, get down. Get down this second."

"Please calm down. I will investigate," answered a man. His words were also in English but they were heavily accented.

Lilith heard a rustle from the bush and this time concentrated on calling forth the poison in her system. She stood over Tarak, deciding that under no circumstances would anyone hurt him again. Not if she could stop it. Glancing down at her hand it practically sparkled.

Then the group was upon them and an Indian man emerged first. He was followed by a middle-aged white couple with two teenage boys in tow. The boys were holding paddles.

The Indian man held both his hands up as a show of faith that he was unarmed. "Are you all right? We heard a gunshot."

He spoke in Hindi and Lilith relaxed. Given the wet suits he and the others were wearing she concluded that he was simply taking these tourists out onto the water for a white water rafting trip.

"You are a guide?"

"Yes. We were ready to head down river where the rapids are not as fierce when we heard the shot. Then we heard someone groaning as if in pain."

"I wasn't groaning that loudly," Tarak said, moaning softly on his way to a sitting position.

Lilith nodded at the guide when it suddenly occurred to her. A guide would take tourists into the jungle for a night of camping and rafting. But he would also have a way to get them out quickly if something happened. That meant transportation.

"A hunter, I believe," she replied back in English, hoping to alleviate the fears of the family behind him. "He shot my…friend. We were out camping. I don't think he saw us."

"Oh, that's just awful. Did you hear that, Bob? He was shot. You need to do something."

Bob's gaze fell to Tarak and immediately he walked over and dropped down on his haunches. Carefully he pulled back the gauze that Lilith had applied and studied the wound.

"It's all right. I'm a doctor."

"He's a doctor," the woman repeated a little louder as if Lilith had not heard the man.

The guide returned his gaze to Lilith. "You were camping? Alone? Out here?"

"Yes," she lied and felt a blush creep over her cheeks. She could only imagine how she looked. Dirty, exhausted and wearing only one silk glove. Lilith glanced down at her hand and was grateful she was no longer shimmering. That might have been harder to explain.

"It was my idea," Tarak interrupted even as Bob began gently prodding around the wound. "Back-to-nature type thing. She didn't want to come at first but I convinced her. Some vacation."

Lilith added nothing to his story, hoping that he'd been convincing enough for the both of them. He was certainly a better liar.

"Well, you're lucky," Bob said as he stood up. "It went through the fleshy part under your arm and clean through your shoulder. Strange, though. It's a rather small bullet for hunting." Bob let that statement hang there for a moment, but then eventually looked at Lilith. "It looks like you've got it cleaned up pretty good but I recommend getting him out of this jungle now before infection sets in."

"Our car is so far back from where we are," Tarak told them. "Would it be possible to have you take us to Bomdila?"

The guide looked back at the family, no doubt trying to determine how they would feel about missing out on their trip and how much of a refund he would have to offer. Lilith practically held her breath waiting for someone to say something when Bob's wife began to nod her head vigorously.

"Of course we'll take you back into town. There's no question. Did you honestly think we would make you walk back to your car in your condition? My goodness! Bob, kids, let's go."

"Oh man! No rafting?" This from the taller of the two teenagers.

"B.J., I don't want to hear another word," his mother scolded. "This man was shot and we have to help him. See…this is why people from other countries don't like Americans. This is our chance to make a good impression and darn it we're going to do it. Now everybody turn back and head for the Jeep."

Two hours later Lilith was walking through an elegant albeit weathered hotel lobby. After so many days in the wild it seemed surreal. The trip into Bomdila had been rather anticlimactic all things considered. What would have taken another day to hike was accomplished in a little less than two hours. As the smallest of the group, Lilith had ridden in the very back of the Land Rover.

Satisfied that there was no way she could touch anyone accidentally and with nothing but time on her hands, Lilith had removed her other glove. Cautiously she'd experimented with calling the poison up and then suppressing it. After two hours it had become almost as simple as flexing a muscle. Remarkable.

"Stay here. I'll get us a room."

Lilith wasn't sure how it was possible that Tarak could function after being shot and then suffering the horribly jostling trip. Still he'd assured Doctor Bob that he would be fine with a little rest and some food as he'd hopped out of the Jeep. The only compensation he'd made was to carry his knapsack on his uninjured shoulder.

While Lilith waited in the center of the lobby she was not ignorant of the looks and whispers by several people milling around the hotel. Feeling more naked than she could ever remember amongst those dressed in more complex saris, she pulled the single glove back on. Not that it helped. It was as dirty and sweat stained as the rest of her.

Normally such things wouldn't have mattered to her. Being clean was something she did because she enjoyed the feeling of it and because it was healthful, not for vanity's sake. But as Tarak turned away from the man behind the counter and looked at her, she thought there were other reasons to be clean. She wondered what he saw when he looked at her. A woman? Or a dirty and spent waif of a girl?

He approached her with a gentle smile on his face. "I secured us a room."

"How?" she wondered. Although she'd never been to a town of this size before she still understood the logistics of how the world worked. A room would cost money.

"A little thing called a credit card. I never leave home without it."

"What do we do now?"

"I'm going to scavenge a bit. Get us some clothes and food. See if I can tell where our friends are and how much time we have."

"I'll go with you."

Tarak shook his head. "No offense, Lilly, but you're a little wilted on the vine. Go up to the room. You can take a shower and rest for a while. I won't be long."

"It's not right. You're hurt. You should wash and rest. I can go and do what needs to be done."

"I'll have an easier way of it. Trust me." He held up a gold plastic card. "You need money, remember."

Defeated on that point, she accepted that he was better equipped to get them what they needed.

"I'll be back shortly," he said. He held up a large metal key. "Open your hand."

Instinctively Lilith held out her gloved hand.

"The other one."

Slowly she raised her uncovered hand.

"Can I touch you?"

Yes. As miraculous and unbelieving as it seemed, she knew she was safe to touch. Smiling, she nodded.

He clasped his hand in hers and for a second they allowed themselves to enjoy the sensation of skin upon skin. His warmth to hers. Then he pressed the key into her hand and closed her fingers over it.

"Room 312. Do you know how to work an elevator?"

"I can take the steps," she said, pointing to where a central staircase led to another floor.

"Be safe. Don't open the door to anyone but me."

"You be safe, as well."

With a hint of a smile he turned and she watched as he left the entrance of the hotel. It was strange. This man whom she had known for only a few days had so quickly become a fixture in her life. His absence was as noticeable to her as the absence of her other glove. It didn't seem logical that she would feel more alone now that he'd gone than she had felt in her whole life. But she did.

He would come back. He'd said so. Then they would find a way to stop Echo together. They were in front of her now so they had more options. They would succeed. Lilith would consider no other outcome.

And then what?

The question knocked her off balance slightly. So much of their journey had been focused around finding and stopping Echo, she hadn't even considered what might happen once they accomplished their goal.

Going back to the village and helping the nuns to rebuild seemed practical. Those needing amputations would still need her medicine. And with her control she might be able to do more. She tried to imagine being back there without Sister Peter. Tried to predict how the people would look at her knowing the trouble she'd inadvertently brought down on their tiny world.

Something told her that going back would not be an option. She couldn't imagine how she would be satisfied with the simple existence that she'd left. Now that she knew control was possible she would need to explore her gift, test the limits and the boundaries of her power. There was more good to be done. More to help than just the people of one leper colony.

Where would she go? How would she function in a world that she knew nothing of? A place where she would need money and access to scientists. She would need someone to show her the way. Would Tarak offer such help? Would he want to take her away with him when he left?

Would she go with him?

His job was to engage in violence. For her own purposes she had used his talents, but staying with him while he fought other people's battles, watching him put himself at risk time and time again, would be torturous.

Too many questions. Lilith put her hands to her head as if to stop the motion of her spinning thoughts. Instead of thinking about things that she had no answers for, she concentrated on finding her room. The steps led to a second floor and then another. One couple came down as she was ascending and her first thought was to move away as she did instinctively when she had to pass people, but this time she forced herself to maintain her normal course.

Not that she had to worry. Upon seeing her, the couple actually made an effort to give her a wide berth. Lilith couldn't help but smile at the idea that it was her smell that was actually more dangerous than her touch in this instance.

She found the room and used the key to unlock the door. Once inside she gasped at the size of the bed. Unable to stop herself, she ran her hand over the soft blanket that was laid out on top. One, two, three, it was almost impossible to count the number of pillows that covered the headboard.

There wasn't much more to the room other than the bed and the pillows, but when she turned into the smaller connected room she found what she knew in theory, if not in practice, to be a bathroom.

Fascinated, she reached for the faucet handle and turned it. Then watched in amazement as the water poured from the spigot. She started to reach for the water then stopped.

"I will not contaminate it. I am not poisonous."

The words helped to steady her and when she looked down at her hand and saw no shimmer she knew the words she spoke were the truth. Thrilled, she ran her hand under the cold water. Of course she knew running water existed, but this was the first time she had ever gotten to use it to bathe.

Turning to her right, she studied the square space closed off with a glass wall. She could see a larger spigot mounted on the wall and another handle below it. Cautiously Lilith reached inside and turned it. She nearly tripped as she stepped backward in surprise. Water poured down over the glass closet. After a moment she found that it heated to the point where it was warm to the touch.

Eager, she stripped out of her now brown silk sheath and stepped naked underneath the spray.

The feeling of water pouring over her skin, through her hair, rinsing away the dirt and the fatigue from her body was like nothing she'd ever felt before.

It was almost as amazing as touching.

Almost.

Chapter 16

Tarak winced as he hoisted his sack over his shoulder, the small motion pulling at the injury. He thought about the purchases that made the pack heavier and very quickly the pain went away. Just thinking about seeing Lilly in the blue sari he'd purchased for her was enough to ease any discomfort. At least the one caused by a bullet hole.

Unfortunately the same image brought with it a new sort of discomfort in a place decidedly south of his shoulder. For the time being, he dismissed that, as well.

After he'd bought the clothes, he found food from a home that basically served the role of a local restaurant. Having subsisted on fruit and jerky the past few days he was anxious for a real meal. The woman who had greeted him seemed to think the same thing as she loaded him up with containers of rice and stewed meat in a pungent curry sauce that made him think of his mother's cooking.

His mouth practically watering at the thought of dinner, he created a mental to-do list as soon as he reached the hotel.

A meal, a shower and then a fashion show. In that order.

And after the fashion show?

It wasn't as if he could stop himself from thinking about it. She was touchable now and that opened the door to all sorts of possibilities. Naturally, as a gentleman, he had to consider what she'd been through the last few days. He should let her eat and sleep.

As a man, he wanted to have her.

It was fair to say that Tarak had no idea which side of him was going to win that battle. He probably wouldn't know until the moment was upon him.

It wasn't as if her fatigue was the only issue he needed to deal with. There was the other thing. Having never been touched before, it was without a doubt that Lilly was a virgin. There was the practical problem it presented. If while in the course of taking her, he hurt her, would that trigger her very deadly defense mechanism? If that did happen, he imagined that there was no better way to die.

Beyond that there was the emotional fallout. What would he do with her after he'd taken her? Send her back to her village to live once again with the nuns and the monks?

Instantly he rejected the idea. The visceral reaction he had to that question was a good indicator that he did not want to give her up. Logically that meant he wanted the opposite: to keep her. Or more accurately, he wanted her to want to keep him. After all, she found him first.

Tarak stopped in front of the hotel as the impact of his thoughts rolled over him like a steamroller. He was a soldier of fortune. A man of violence, as Lilly liked to call him. He'd spent the first part of his adult life chasing down the people responsible for his parents' deaths. Once he'd accomplished that the only option left to him was to keep on fighting, to use his unique skills in the best way he could.

He thought he'd carved out a nice little niche for himself. Now that life seemed empty. Honestly, he'd felt that way long before the betrayal in Colombia.

That's why he'd returned to India, to his mother's people. He'd come back to retrace his steps. To start over again from a common point. Yes, he'd lived most of his life in London, but this was where his parents met. This was where they fell in love. This was where he'd been born.

He'd come back to the beginning to find a new course and he'd stumbled upon Lilly.

He thought of his mother and how happy she would have been that he'd found a nice Indian girl to wed. It made him smile.

From there everything fell into place. There would be no going back for Lilith. Only forward with him. He knew it in his gut. He imagined she might balk when he told her what her future would be, but she would come around to see things his way. He was certain of it.

Increasing the speed of his steps despite the pain in his shoulder, Tarak took the stairs leading up to the third floor two at a time. He had his own key and used it to let himself in the room. He set his bag down then froze when he didn't see Lilly in the small room.

The sound of running water gave her away. He walked over to the bathroom and stepped inside the open door. The room was filled with hot steam and beyond the glass door he could see his future bride in all her splendid glory. Her hair fell like a black sheet down her back, sticking to her body in a way that suggested her hair knew a good thing when it found it.

He thought about the first time he'd seen her just like this and decided he would never grow tired of watching this woman bathe.-

"How long have you been in there?"

Startled, Lilith turned and then sheepishly lowered her head. "How long have you been gone?"

"Almost a half hour." He laughed. "You're going to turn into a prune."

"It's so wonderful. And it stays hot."

"Well, I imagine the rest of the hotel will be out of luck, but who cares. Step aside and I'll join you."

Tarak stepped out of his boots and socks and then carefully slid his T-shirt up and over his head, gently pulling it down his arm. He reached for the buckle on his pants and stopped. When he looked up, she was staring at him in a way he'd never been stared at before.

There was curiosity in her gaze, mixed with need. Possibly desire, too, although he imagined she had a hard time understanding what that was. But there was also trust. Blinding in its purity. It humbled him and filled him with a renewed sense of purpose.

"Have you ever seen a man, Lilly?"

"Of course."

"You know what I mean."

"I… From a distance."

"This won't be from a distance. I'll be in the shower with you. Touching you. And then eventually I'll come inside you. There will be no distance." Tarak bade a fond farewell to his gentleman half. He'd never had much use for him anyway.

"Yes," was all she managed.

Tarak shucked off his pants. He knew he was hard already but he figured that was part of it. She needed to become accustomed to all of him. He opened the shower door and she took a step back. He could see her gaze fall to his erection and then watched as she tried not to stare.

"It will hurt a little. But only the first time. You need to trust me or this won't work."

"I do trust you."

The hot water hit him and for a second he let the heat wash over him. He would need to rebandage his wound later but for now he felt no pain. The water pelted his body and he tilted his head back to wet his hair.

He felt her tiny hand rest in the center of his chest and knew that this encounter would be more important than anything he'd ever done.

He lowered his gaze to where she was touching him and then met her eyes.

"I touched you," she whispered. "First."

"Yes. I like it very much."

"You're beautiful."

"Hardly. But I'm glad you think so. Turn around and close your eyes. I think it will be easier for you to just feel at first. These sensations are going to be very strong, Lilly. Do you understand? I don't want you to be frightened by them."

"I understand."

Only she didn't. Not at all. Obediently, Lilith turned around and closed her eyes. She knew why he was concerned that she understand what was about to happen, but she had no worries about hurting him. She was in control of her body now, and this was what she wanted. She didn't think it possible that she would ever be able to hurt him.

Then she felt his hands slide around her waist. He pulled her back against his chest and she felt the solid muscle of his body covered with dark hair pressing against her. His erection pushed into her lower back as he made no effort to shield her from it. Wet hands drifted up from her waist and covered her breasts. Pure fire rocketed from her breasts to her belly and down farther until her knees buckled.

"It's…too much. It…hurts."

"No," he rumbled in her ear, taking the time to nip it. "It's not pain that you're feeling. It's pleasure. Concentrate."

Concentrate. How was that possible? Her body was awash with such powerful sensations she couldn't form a coherent thought. All at once she felt his tongue on her neck while his fingers pinched the very tips of her breasts, turning them into hard little points. One hand continued to linger over her body and she could feel the scrape of his teeth where his tongue had just been. Then another hand drifted lower, cupping her between her legs.

For moments he held her still. One hand on her breast, the other on her sex. She thought this alone might have been enough to shatter her. To rip her body apart with electricity. But then his hand slipped farther between her legs, his fingers playing with the folds of her sex. Dipping inside her then out. Then deeper inside. Then out.

She could feel a heavy wetness where his fingers stroked that she knew wasn't a result of the shower. The slickness allowed his fingers deeper access. Dazed with pleasure, Lilith considered how perfect nature was in that regard. Making a man hard so that he could penetrate and a woman soft so that she could accept him.

As if from a distance she could hear herself moaning and sighing. The sounds she made were like nothing she'd ever heard before. Primitive noises that erupted from her without consciousness. She wouldn't have believed it was her making them, but the only other sound she heard was Tarak's harsh breathing behind her.

Her hips rocked on his wonderful hand without shame. It was as if there was a string inside her that he'd found and captured with his fingers. A string he continued to pull on harder and harder until it was so tight inside her body she was sure it would snap.

And then it did.

A warm, terrible wave of satisfaction started in her belly and spread out to every nerve in her system. It was unfathomable how completely good it felt. She arched against him, her buttocks riding the hard ridge of his erection, urging him to do more. Take more.

A drift of an idea passed through her brain and she realized that this was the way of mating. The wanting first, then the urge, until it all became need. She was his to take, and she was calling him to do so. Silently begging for him to finish this. Just as nature intended. It did not matter what the species…even for a freak like her.

"I wanted to take you on the bed," he said harshly in her ear. "I thought it would be easier for you, but I can't.… I have to…"

He didn't finish his sentence. Instead he lifted her leg high so that her thigh was draped over his arm. She could feel him lean over her and then suddenly he was there—hard and thick, pressing against her center. She braced her hands against the tile wall and felt him, inch by inch, slip farther inside her body. His lips kissed the spot where her neck met her back while his hips thrust against her in what was becoming a compelling rhythm.

This time he was making the noises, grunting softly as he tried to push himself farther inside her body, and she found that the harder she pushed against the wall the deeper he went.

At first there had been a pinching. Now there was fullness. A tightness that almost bordered on pain. But she couldn't separate the pain from the pleasure that was still riding her system. His hand covered hers on the tile wall. She could see the muscles in his arm were strained. The speed of his thrusts began to increase and his grip on her thigh tightened. He'd promised her that there would be no distance and he'd been right.

She was being touched. Inside and out. He was everywhere. Around her and in her. It was more spiritually fulfilling than anything the monks had ever taught her.

"Tarak," she whispered even as his shout echoed through the small shower stall. He stilled then and she felt a pulsing deep inside her body. Then she heard his soft sighs and felt his muscles relax. The grip he had on her hand eased. Slowly he separated his body from hers and let her leg drop to the floor.

Tears filled her eyes but she had no explanation for them.

He turned her then, and placed her arms around his neck, holding her tightly to him. "I'm sorry," he muttered. "So sorry, my little flower."

Enchanted by the simple hug, it took a moment for her to understand his words.

"Why?"

He pulled back and wiped a tear from her cheek. "I should have been easier with you. Gentler."

He bent to kiss her, his lips pressing against hers. That sensation was as startling as the others. And just as lovely.

"I've taken you, but yet I've not kissed your mouth."

Lilith glanced up at him. "You can kiss it now, can't you?"

He smiled although she wasn't sure why. Someday she would make him explain his sense of humor, but not right now. "Yes. I can kiss it now. But first we need to get out of this shower before we both shrivel up."

He helped her out of the stall and took his time drying her body with the fluffy towels. Such luxury, she thought. Then it was her turn. First, she dried his body, and then, because his wound had begun to bleed again, she cleaned it and rebandaged it.

"It must have hurt your shoulder," she said as she covered the wound with what was left of the gauze in his first-aid kit. "Moving like you were."

"Trust me. I wasn't feeling anything in my shoulder."

"Still, we will wait before we do that again."

"Again?" He raised a single brow above his eye. Lilith touched it gently. She thought of Sister Peter and how she used to have the same trick. She thought about what Sister Peter might think of Lilith's behavior, but in her heart she knew the sister would be happy for her.

In a way, that simple expression made Lilith realize that her friend would always be there in her heart. It helped to let the guilt go.

"Of course," Lilith answered adamantly. "It was quite…wonderful. Did you not think?"

This time he laughed full heartedly and then, with his good arm, he pulled her closer so that he could kiss her again. "I did think it. My only regret is not being easier with you and not doing everything I wanted to do."

Lilith's eyes widened. "There is more?"

"Much more. A whole lifetime of more. But first we'll eat and then we should sleep."

"Yes."

It was time to return to the reality of their situation. While the respite was lovely there was still a goal to be accomplished. She needed to retrieve the necklace. She thought about the data on the flash drive, the files that she hadn't told Tarak about. The blackmail and the money and the evil people who held such powerful positions.

She knew now that she would have to tell him everything. If somehow they failed in getting it back, at least if he knew the power that Echo was wielding, he might find another way to stop her.

There would be time for that tomorrow, though. Tonight was unquestionably theirs.

Back in the room, dressed only in a towel, Tarak laid sprawled out on the bed as he began to show off the rice and stewed meat he'd purchased. Lilith secured another of the towels around her and for a second hesitated before joining him on the bed.

It was probably silly, but the sense of intimacy was still very new and unsettling.

"Come. I have a feast for you."

Thinking that she would have to adjust eventually, Lilith walked over to the bed and joined him.

"You hesitate," he noted absently as he scooped up some seasoned rice with his fingers and dropped it into his mouth. "I know you're not afraid of me anymore. You couldn't be. And I know you're not afraid of hurting me. So why?"

It was hard to put into words. The fear she'd had earlier in the day about what would happen when this was over. The certainty that her life had changed, but having no idea what direction she was headed next and whether she would head in that direction alone or with him.

"I do not want you to kill people anymore."

Tarak lifted his head, his expression somber. "I might have to kill one more person. Maybe a few...to get you your necklace back."

"I understand that, but after."

"After." He nodded. "We'll need to spend some time talking about *after* when this is over. I have some ideas about it myself. But right now we need to focus on the present. We need to get our strength back, rest a little and then formulate yet another plan."

Lilith sat on the bed and reached for some of the meat. The taste exploded on her tongue and her stomach quickly realized how long it had been since it had been fed. But the flavor wasn't nearly as compelling as Tarak's mouth.

"You know where she is."

"Yes," he answered. "I've still got her on my receiver. And I spoke with some of the locals. There is a path that she should eventually find. It will bring her into the city from the northeast. Then if we have it right, she'll take the train to New Delhi."

"And what will we do?"

"We will already be on the train. And when we get to the city we'll have a friend waiting for us."

"You have already made contact?"

"I sent an e-mail. I expect a reply soon."

"This friend will have more friends, I hope."

Tarak chuckled. "That's my girl. Always focused on the objective. She'll have friends. Once we meet up with her we'll find a way to tail Echo. My guess is she'll try to leave the city so the most likely place will be the airport."

"Do we want to let her get that close to escape? Why not try to take her out on the train?"

"Because I still haven't figured out how to get past her trick." He sighed. "And the safer she feels, the more she'll relax her guard and the better chance we'll have to take her by surprise. Maybe she knew we were coming in the jungle when there was only us to contend with, but Delhi is a different place altogether."

Lilith nodded, satisfied that she could leave the planning in his hands while she ate. When they were full, he stretched out on the bed and removed his towel, as comfortable with his nudity as he was dressed in all black.

He patted the space next him. "Come here. I can't take you again or I'll hurt you, but we can sleep together like lovers. You'll enjoy that."

But Lilith shook her head. "I should not."

"Please, we've been through this. Now that you have control you don't have to worry about hurting me."

"Awake I have control. If something happened. If Echo found us. I could wake and react without knowing it. I'll sleep on the floor."

Tarak growled and sat up. "I'll sleep on the floor, damn it. I've sacrificed the gentleman part of me once already today. I won't do it a second time."

"But your wound. You should have the bed."

His eyes narrowed as he moved to stand very close. "Lilith, if you don't get your pretty little ass on that bed I'm going to spank it and this time I can back up my threat."

Lilith felt a jolt in the pit of her stomach. "Why does your saying that make me feel jittery inside instead of fearful?"

Closing his eyes, he groaned softly as if her words had hurt him.

"Let's just say that was some of the *more* I was talking about. But in this case it should make you fearful rather than jittery. I'm very serious. Now to bed. We only have a few hours before we need to leave for the train station."

With a shrug of acceptance, Lilith traded places. She

gave Tarak some pillows and the top blanket and then she, too, slid out of her towel and underneath the fresh sheets. Never had she felt such softness as she did when she sank into the thick mattress. This time she was the one groaning and it definitely was not in pain. So many sensations she'd experienced today. So much pleasure. For fun she moaned again as she wiggled deeper into the bed.

"Lilith."

"Yes, Tarak?"

"I say this with all due respect.... Please shut up."

A sense of understanding settled over Lilith. Now was not the time to taunt him.

"Yes, Tarak."

Chapter 17

Allison read the message off her computer screen for the third time before she allowed herself to believe it. Even then she still didn't believe it.

"Because it's unbelievable," she said to an empty office.

It seemed as if one of her Oracle contacts, Lucy Karmon, had gotten a message from an old acquaintance. She was being asked to fly to New Delhi to help stop a woman from escaping with a valuable and potentially dangerous necklace.

A woman with strange abilities.

Allison shook her head as she considered the information. Was it possible that Echo had literally fallen into her lap?

If that was the case it almost seemed too easy. Her

search had started with two locations. South Africa and India. It was easy enough to find Jackie's first daughter. Her name: Echo. No last name.

Reports of a female, the right age, with a long history of illegal activity, not to mention strange talents, had immediately gotten a hit during Oracle's data search. Apparently Jackie's daughter had already established a fearsome criminal reputation in Johannesburg. Wanting to build on that intel, Allison had used her contacts to scour South Africa for more information on Echo. Her agents had been able to locate places Echo had been, learned of several people she had murdered and a lot of money she had stolen. But no one could tell her where she was.

But the other one in India—there was simply no trace of her. No leads on a woman with strange or unique powers. At least none that showed up through the normal information channels. This led Allison to believe she had simply gone into hiding. That or maybe she had no idea who she was or what she could do. With so many unknowns, it was hard to make assumptions.

But now this. A woman with strange powers shows up in India and obviously steals something highly valuable. Given her history, the likely thief was Echo. The question was who was chasing her and why?

Allison minimized Lucy's message and brought up another window. Quickly she did some preliminary research on Tarak Hammer-Smith. She wasn't sure whether to be pleased or nervous by what she found.

Like Lucy the man was a mercenary for hire. Follow-

ing his father's path, he started his career in the British
military before signing on with MI6. A few years later
he left the agency. An ex-MI6 agent with a grudge? Or
maybe someone like Lucy who hadn't been able to work
well within a system?

Allison continued to read and discovered that it had
been shortly after the deaths of his parents in a car
bombing that Hammer-Smith had decided to quit the
British agency to work independently. It didn't take a
great logical leap to realize what had driven him away.

Curious, she wondered if he'd ever found the terrorists who murdered his family.

Then she looked at his assignments for the past
several years. For the most part, he'd worked as a
contract agent for British or U.S. intelligence. In some
cases even for the U.S. military.

She was going to have to assume he was one of the
good guys. So, good guy Tarak Hammer-Smith finds
himself back in India chasing a woman with unique
skills who has stolen a necklace. How does a man not
involved in a situation—Allison could find no links
between Echo's criminal activity and Tarak's past
assignments—become involved with a situation?

Because someone asks him to. Someone he might
care about. Someone from his country of birth?

The scenarios played around in Allison's head for a
time. She was making huge leaps based on only frag-
mented information but if she arranged the pieces in the
correct pattern they told a reasonable story. Jackie sends

out three packages. One to Kwan-Sook, one to Echo and another to her daughter in India. Kwan-Sook is dead, her package stolen. Echo leaves South Africa and turns up in India where it appears another package, a necklace, has been stolen.

Allison could say for certain that Tarak wasn't Jackie's daughter, therefore it stood to reason that he was helping to get it back for the person who had lost it.

Arachne's third child.

If all that were true the next question was why did Jackie's third child want it back? Was she battling Echo for superiority or did she know what was on the files and know how dangerous they were?

Lucy was waiting on the other end of cyberspace for an answer. A call had to be made and Allison had really nothing more than instinct to tell her what to do. Trusting her gut, Allison tabbed back to the other window and replied to Lucy, giving her an update of the events she would need to be aware of if she was going to help her friend.

"Right time. Right place. Possibly the right man. Or the right woman," Allison muttered aloud. "All I can hope for is that you're one of the good guys, whoever you are."

Lucy glanced down at her PalmPilot. "Yeah, I thought you would be interested in that little piece of information. Okay. You're the boss."

She replied to the message and then pocketed the

PalmPilot. Lucy leaned against a wall and tried to look inconspicuous among an airport full of tourists and travelers passing through Rome. Not the easiest thing for a tall redhead to do, but she'd taught herself to become an expert at blending into her surroundings.

There was no question about where she was headed. She had already made up her mind to join Tarak in India before she'd sent the e-mail. A call for help from a friend wasn't something she ignored.

Not that Nolan was thrilled. They'd just settled down into a nice homey routine and here she was off on another mission before they'd had a chance to calm down from the events of the last one.

He'd wanted to come along, but Lucy had protested, insisting this would be a quick in-and-out gig. Get in and get out. See what she could do for Tarak and then head back to Nolan as fast as possible.

Besides, she had something personal to discuss with Tarak that she was sure he would want to hear directly from her. After setting up some additional muscle that would be waiting for her when she arrived in New Delhi, Lucy settled down for the interminable waiting that was indicative of airline travel.

Arachne had daughters, she thought, recalling the e-mailed reply. How crazy was that?

"Will we know when she is on the train?" Lilith asked.

Tarak glanced at his receiver. "Yes. But after that the blip will essentially be on top of us. We won't know if she's three cars back or sitting directly across from us, although I expect we might notice if that was the case."

Lilith nodded. Her heart was racing faster than it ever had in the jungle, in the anticipation that the end of their journey was close.

This morning she'd woken up to find Tarak standing over her, a gentle smile on his face. She returned the smile, sensing what he was feeling and returning the emotions. Without words, he'd expressed everything she'd needed to know. So much so that she was no longer worried about her future.

Their future.

He'd slid into the bed with her and spent time simply kissing her and holding her. Tickling her and caressing her. Getting her used to the sensations she'd experienced the night before. Making it easier for her to accept his touches. But when she'd asked for more he'd resisted. Time was passing, he'd told her. And he'd convinced her that time was a critical element in order to show her *more*.

Instead she'd dressed in the sari he'd provided. It was a rich-looking gown with beads hand sewn into the vibrantly blue material. In her life she'd never seen anything as beautiful, but beyond that she'd never considered any clothing other than the encompassing silk material that had been her uniform for as long as she could remember.

He'd helped her arrange the petticoat and sari so that it draped over her right shoulder and then he'd made her turn around. Twice.

She thought he might have been checking to see if it was secure, but his mischievous smile when she turned around for the second time told another story entirely.

The sari wasn't the only article of clothing he'd purchased for her. There were gloves, too. Silk gloves that she could pull up to her elbows. The relief of having them despite her newfound control brought tears to her eyes. So much had changed for her in such a short time. When he'd given her the gloves, he'd given her more than protection in case something should happen—he'd given her a sense of connection to who she was as well as to where she was going.

Looking down at her gloved hands, she was reminded of that all over again. He understood that she needed these as a barrier against the world that she was only just beginning to rejoin. At least for now.

"Stop fidgeting," he scolded, reaching down to take one of her hands. "There is nothing to do but enjoy the passing scenery."

Lilith sniffed. "And to worry about whether Echo is even on the train. Worry that we've correctly identified where she is going. Worry that if we have guessed correctly and she is on the train that she will spot us. Worry about what will happen if she does."

"That's a lot of worrying. All things you can't control. Relax. You look like a beautiful Indian bride and I am your husband. We're simply traveling together on this trip to Delhi. I doubt Echo is concerned with us at this point, but I suspect she would not realize who we were if she sat on top of us. Look around you. We look exactly like everyone else."

Lilith took a sly glance around the train car. There was a mother and her child sitting across from them. The train was crowded with travelers. So crowded that others stood in the aisle. How strange, she thought. She did look like them. Her skin was lighter perhaps. And the color of her eyes. But here she was on a train with so many people and no one suspected that she was different.

She wondered if there would come a time, if she lived in this world long enough, that she would forget she was different.

"There we go," Tarak said, bringing Lilith out of her musings. "The blip is on top of us. Looks like sis made the train."

"What do you mean do I have a ticket? Of course I have a ticket. I have a ticket right here." Echo pulled out a gun and held it against the belly of the man who apparently was the train's ticket collector.

"Please," he whispered to her in Hindi. "I don't want to die."

"I don't understand what you're saying," Echo answered. "And I don't care. You're going to turn around and leave me and my two friends here alone for the duration of this trip. I have had a very long hike. I'm tired. I'm dirty. I'm hungry. When I'm tired and dirty and hungry I get cranky. You understand cranky?"

The man nodded quickly.

"Wonderful. Now run along."

He turned and walked back down the aisle of the train not once asking anyone else for a ticket. Echo imagined he might try to report her, but she wasn't worried. They wouldn't stop the train so the worst that might happen would be that she would have to dodge some authorities when they got to New Delhi.

Glancing at the car, she could see there were no seats available. In fact, most of the people were stuffed into the center aisle like sheep. Turning to her left, she could see an older man staring at her. His eyes were wide with fear.

"Saw the gun, did you? Good. Then you know I'll kill you if you don't get up and give me that seat."

Immediately the man sprang from the seat and pulled the woman who was sitting next to him with him.

"Excellent," Echo crooned. "Such gracious people in this country." She took the vacated seat and put her legs up on the other one preventing either Rolf or Kent from sitting next to her. After several days in the jungle they reeked.

"What next?" Kent wanted to know.

In her mind, Echo imagined herself waiting until she boarded the plane to get the hell out of India and then, at the last possible second, killing both of them. Her initial thoughts to keep Rolf alive were foolish. Anyone who knew what Lilith could do had to die. It was as simple as that. But she figured it wasn't the best time to tell them that what was next...was killing them.

"Next we get to New Delhi and we get on a plane. I

want a private one. As soon as we have cell reception get on that."

"They cost money," Kent pointed out.

The man really was brainless, she decided. "Really? Money." Pulling out the necklace that she'd taken to wearing around her neck Echo held it up to him. "Do you know how much this is worth? Any idea?"

And since he would be dead before long it didn't matter that she was going to tell them.

"Billions. No, more than that. Maybe all of the world's wealth if I want it. It's official. My mother's empire is now mine. Mine. Mine. Mine. This obviously proves that I was the cream of her particular crop. You know what I've decided, boys? I'm going to hatch my own little offspring. Maybe a whole army of women with my skills and, of course, my killer smile."

"I don't give a shit what you do. I just want to get paid," Kent said.

"You'll get everything I promised. Maybe if you're a very good boy and don't whine for the rest of the trip, I'll give you a bonus."

Kent didn't bother to reply. Instead he braced his legs apart to keep his balance as the train rocked its way out of the station. Rolf bent down close to Echo.

"I would gladly offer my services to be the father of your children."

Echo patted his cheek. "Sweet boy. Yes, it seems I'm going to have to give you a bonus, too. Now go away from me. You smell."

Immediately he backed away from her, obviously
upset by her dismissal. Weak. Echo couldn't imagine
why she'd hired these two in the first place. Once she
was back in South Africa it would be different. There
she would carefully build her army. Handpicking only
the most loyal, the most qualified.

The most deadly.

Closing her eyes, she allowed herself to imagine how
it would be. She'd build a palace for herself. Certainly
that would be her first order of business. Given what
happened to her mother, security was paramount.

Then she would take a look at the world and determine where she wanted to strike first. Which president
of which nation would she expose as an example to the
rest? Which would she then choose to dangle over her
particular pit of hell?

Oh, the fun she was going to have.

Suddenly a tingle on the back of her neck alerted her.
She opened her eyes to find nothing had changed. Kent
and Rolf stood in front of where she sat. There was still
a crush of people around them, all of them now jostling
as the train moved.

A flash of Lilith's face entered her mind, but instantly she squashed it. There was no way the insipid
creature had managed to find her way out of the forest.
Not without her man. If Echo had to guess, they were
still stuck where she'd left them. Him with a bullet in
his body and her probably wringing her hands fretfully
wondering what she should do.

Echo knew she was eventually going to have to go back to kill Lilith. It was the only way to ensure that Jackie's empire would remain hers. Not that she was worried that Lilith presented any further threat. If the bitch showed gumption by coming after her it was nothing more troubling than a fly buzzing at an elephant's head.

But the idea of the two of them living in the same world didn't sit well with Echo.

She would get back to Jo'burg and hire a team of mercenaries. A hundred if she had to. They would hunt Lilith down and kill her.

She would have them bring her Lilith's head. Isn't that what all the queens used to do with their enemies?

Echo smiled. Queen Echo. It really had a rather nice ring to it.

"We're almost there."

Lilith heard the whisper in her ear and popped her eyes open. She glanced out at the window and saw a rush of people standing on the other side of the tracks. Then her eyes spotted the buildings. So many buildings of different shapes and sizes. Silver and gold and brick. And there were automobiles on the streets. Driving alongside people pushing carts and selling all manner of things. Men argued. Women hustled their children from place to place. Dogs barked frantically.

These sights. In her life she'd never seen such things.

"So many people," she whispered. It was one thing to be on the train with people. Sitting next to Tarak she felt insulated. But out there, walking around with all of these people, she would be crushed. "I do not think I can do this. I have never seen anything like this. What if I bump into someone? Fall or trip and I cannot stop my reaction. What if…"

"Calm down," Tarak tightened his grip on her hand. "Remember, you're in control."

Lilith nodded. She took several breaths and tried to focus on why she was here.

"Echo."

"Yes. We need to find her. Stop her. And get the necklace back. As soon as we do, we'll leave. I promise."

Again Lilith nodded. She could do this. She had to do this. The train eventually came to a stop. Slowly the people began to debark until finally it was time for Lilith and Tarak to stand. Carefully she looked around her. Obviously Echo was not in their train car, but they knew she was close. They needed to get off the train without being spotted by her or her men.

"You think she will go to the airport right away?"

"I do," Tarak said. "Now that she has all the pieces to her puzzle, I imagine she'll want to put them together."

Keeping her head down, Lilith followed Tarak as he tugged on her hand to lead her off the train. It didn't take them long to get outside the station to the busy street. He stopped her for a moment and again she had to control the panic that seemed to want to envelop her. What she'd seen from the train had only been a small portion of the activity that was around her.

How did these people live together like this? How was it possible that a defined space could hold so many lives? If she had to imagine all the people in the world, she didn't think there would be as many as this.

"Stay close."

"That will not be a problem," she assured him. "What are we waiting for?"

"Our ride."

As he said the words a compact car zipped its way between two other cars on the road nearly sideswiping a food cart along the way. The brakes squeaked as the car stopped just short of where Tarak was standing.

The driver rolled down the dirt-smeared window and inside Lilith could see there was a redheaded woman behind the wheel.

"Need a lift, mister?"

"Please tell me you didn't come alone."

The redhead smiled. "What? You need more than me on this job? I don't know, T. I think you're getting soft in your old age."

"I am only a year older than you."

"Right. Get in. My people are already in position."

Tarak opened the door and tilted the seat forward so that Lilith could slip into the back. He took the passenger seat in front and shut the door.

"Lucy Karmon, this is Lilith," Tarak introduced. "Lilith, this is Lucy."

"Your friend," Lilith said, for her own peace of mind.

"I hope she is my friend," Tarak said quietly. "Well?

I need to know, Lucy. Before we go any further. Did you betray me?"

Lucy turned her head to face him, shaking her head in obvious disgust. "You know, you really should have asked me that before you got into the car."

Chapter 18

Lilith didn't exactly understand what was happening, but she sensed that Lucy might be a threat. Immediately she began to pull off her glove. This woman would not hurt Tarak. Even as the glove came free she could see the shine on her skin and knew that she was armed.

"It's all right, Lilith. You don't have to hurt her."

"Hurt me?" Lucy looked over her shoulder into the backseat. "She was going to hurt me with her hand?"

"She has a rather unique touch," Tarak said. "I'm sorry, Lucy. I had to ask. You provided the intel for that mission. You must have heard what happened."

"I did. And when I didn't hear from you after I knew things went south, I got the feeling that it must have been with the intelligence, that maybe you suspected me. You could have asked me, Tarak."

"I was sort of busy trying to get out of Colombia alive, when I did I didn't know who to trust. I was lost. Physically, spiritually."

"But you called me," Lucy reminded him. "You asked for my help."

"Call it a gut hunch. I am relying on those a lot these days."

Lucy smiled. "Good hunch. It wasn't me. Now you want the good news?"

"Please."

"Vasher is dead."

"You?"

"Unnecessary. As is typical in these types of trans-actions, after they hired him to give you false informa-tion they decided that rather than paying him they could kill him for much less."

"When will the traitors ever learn?" Tarak turned around and smiled reassuringly at Lilith. "It's all right. She's a friend."

"I agree with her. We should have verified that before we got in the car." Annoyed, Lilith sat back against the seat and tried not to look at the chaos that was passing all around her. People on bicycles moved at fast speeds, weaving between the cars. It was a miracle that they weren't constantly being hit.

Or perhaps they were. Lilith couldn't say what it might feel like to be hit by a motorized vehicle. Perhaps a bump here and there didn't make a difference to the riders. They must be used to it.

"She's feisty, Tarak. Who is she?"

"Lilith is a friend who is currently having…family troubles."

"Family troubles?" Lucy snorted. "Look, Tarak, I get the only-what-you-need-to-know-keep-everything-vague thing, but I left a really warm bed, a *really* warm bed, to be here. For you. So I need to know. Everything."

"Then I will explain.…"

Again Lilith found herself irritated by the conversation happening in the front of the car. "I can speak English. I also understand that it is rude to discuss someone as if they are not present. I am here. I am the person who has the problem. The person who brought Tarak into this. It is my favor to ask. My responsibility."

"Sorry, love," Tarak muttered. "You're right. You tell her."

Lilith didn't miss the surprising look that Lucy gave Tarak. But as much as the woman would have liked to continue staring at him in shock a large bus was headed seemingly directly at them. She swerved the vehicle and made an odd gesture with her hand out the window as the bus passed. After that, she kept her eyes pinned to the road in front of her.

Lilith found herself trying to formulate the story she wanted to tell. When she listened to it in her head, even she didn't believe her. It all seemed so unreal. But it wasn't. That was the truly ridiculous thing.

Finally she said, "My half sister has taken something from me that I need to get back." It was the easy truth.

"Okay. I get that. Tarak said this half sister of yours has special talents."

"She does. She can block things."

"Things?"

"Bullets. People. It is a field that she can create around herself. Although I cannot say if the field covers her completely. I do not know how she creates it, how long it will last or if there is anything that can penetrate it."

"Well, that pretty much sums it up."

There was silence for a time and Lilith tried to assess what the woman meant. She feared Lucy was using sarcasm and while Lilith understood what the word meant she was not the best at interpreting it.

"You think I am lying?"

"No. I don't."

"If you believe me then you do not seem as surprised as I might have expected. As if you already know that such things are possible."

Lilith could see the woman shrug her shoulders. "Let's just say I've seen my share of strange and unusual things in this world."

"No," Tarak countered as he stared at his friend. "It is more than that. Do you know who Lilith is looking for?"

"We're here at the airport. Let's get settled and then I'll explain everything."

Lucy turned the wheel and Lilith fell sideways as the car made a harsh turn into the entrance to the city's airport. All things considered, Lilith concluded that she would rather be hiking through the jungle.

Less dangerous.

"They're searching the train," Rolf reported.

"So?" Echo pushed past Rolf and a few other travelers who had been asked to remain inside the train car. Instead she made her way to where the exit door was still sealed shut. Turning around, she caught Kent's eye.

"Come here and shoot it."

He muscled his way to where she stood near the sliding glass. A latch mechanism sealed it from the other side. "Shoot through the glass and I'll open it from the other side."

"You don't think that might arouse some suspicion?"

"You think I care? I want out of this country. I want my plane. I want to go home. What's stopping me is this door and, currently, you. Now I don't want to waste my bullets, but I know you have plenty of them so shoot the glass."

Kent sighed but moved her back a few steps. As soon as the first bullet left his gun Echo could see everyone in the train car in front of them hit the deck. Including the police who were checking each row of seats. Behind her, the crush of people started to cry and shout as they, too, tried to make themselves smaller by crouching low. Only there wasn't nearly enough room for that. Irritated, Echo didn't lash out; instead she focused on getting off the train.

Three more shots and there was a decent enough size hole in the glass. Forming a shield around her fist, she punched through the glass and opened the latch from the outside. The door slid open and she could almost smell it: home. But then she smelled the crowded streets of New Delhi. "This doesn't smell good at all," she whined.

It wouldn't be long now, she told herself. One last journey, some minor details and she would be off to conquer the world.

"Hold it right there!"

Echo stopped as what passed for a police officer in this city held up his hand. She realized her expression must have been lacking in respect, because he scowled and drew out a long stick with a metal tip on the top. The *lathi,* an ancient weapon, was still the sidearm of choice for the Indian police and it almost made her laugh.

Actually she would have laughed if she hadn't been so annoyed at being delayed. But this was no longer funny.

"Back off."

The officer could obviously see she wasn't threatened and reached for his sidearm. A small sidearm that he had trouble dislodging from his holster. He turned his head and shouted in Hindi for his comrades.

Echo wasn't fazed. She merely hopped down the steps to the platform. The man backed off, clearly uncertain what to do with such a recalcitrant criminal. When he finally dislodged the small gun Echo put her hands on her face and blinked a few times.

"Oh, no! The policeman is going to shoot me."

"Do not move," he shouted in English, his eyes wider than an ocean. "Or I will shoot."

Echo looked behind her to find Rolf and Kent stationed securely behind her back. Of course that was where they would be. They knew a good thing when they saw it.

"Okay."

She took a deliberate step forward. Then another. Then another. The gun that waggled in the policeman's hand started to dip, and then suddenly, as if he understood his life was in danger, he tightened his grip. He raised the weapon. Pointed it directly at her heart.

And pulled the trigger.

The bullet exploded out of the gun with extreme force. Echo knew she'd have little time to construct her field but she wasn't worried. Her thoughts could travel faster than a bullet and that was all it took.

She could see a ripple of impact and then the projectile was ricocheting into another direction. She wasn't sure where until the man ten feet down on the platform to her left, who must have been waiting for one of the passengers to disembark, suddenly clutched his arm and fell to his knees. The man shouted as blood poured between his fingers.

"Oops. Looks like you missed."

The policeman was clearly stunned by the chain of events. He twisted the gun so that the nozzle faced toward him no doubt expecting something to have happened to it. Echo wondered if he thought she might have bent the thing in half with her mind.

Now that would be a talent.

Instead he froze as she continued to walk toward him and calmly removed the gun from his hand.

"You shot an innocent bystander. Tsk, tsk, tsk. You are going to be in *trouble*."

Beyond understanding, the man had nothing to say in return. He turned his eyes in the direction of the fallen man whom the other officers had rushed to in order to administer first aid. Without warning the officer's legs gave out and he plopped down ass-first on the concrete platform.

"Next time you'll remember this when someone tells you to back off. Let's go, boys. We have a plane to catch."

"You're in position?"

Lilith listened to a voice reply over the phone—a phone that didn't ring but beeped instead—that he was indeed in position. Curious, Lilith glanced around the parking lot of the airport where they were now waiting and tried to determine if she could see where this position was.

"You know what we're looking for. Two muscle, one woman. She's going to be calling the shots, but no way of knowing how loyal they'll be to her if the bullets start flying. We could get lucky and they might back off."

"Yes, because in our work we get lucky so often," Tarak drawled.

Lucy glared at him but didn't reply. Instead she put the handheld phone down on the console between them and met Lilith's obviously worried gaze through the rearview mirror.

"You can relax—we've got everything covered. I've

got five people scattered throughout the airport and another five at key spots."

"What is a key spot?"

"At terminals for two airline flights leaving for South Africa plus the private jets terminal. I already know two planes have been reserved. They won't tell me where they're going, but if it was me and I was trying to get out of Dodge I might want a little more control over my schedule."

Lilith shook her head. "I don't understand…dodge. What is she dodging?"

"Forget it. Just know that I'm as keen as you are to talk to your sister. As soon as we get a nibble we'll move."

"You never explained how you knew who she was," Tarak pointed out.

Lucy shrugged. "That's a little complicated. And I don't know Echo. I know of her."

"You know her name," Lilith said. It was difficult not to feel suspicion again. How was it possible that this woman who was just supposed to be a friend to Tarak could know that name?

"I recently learned her name. I also happen to have a passing acquaintance with your mother."

This time Lilith had no trouble deciphering Lucy's meaning. The memory obviously wasn't a fond one.

"I know what my mother was. I know what Echo is. There is no point in protecting me. What I do not know is how you are a part of this."

Lucy nodded. "Okay. That's fair. Have you ever

heard of a place called the Athena Academy? Or of a woman named Allison Gracelyn?"

The name instantly registered with Lilith, but it took her a few moments to place it in context. Then she remembered. "She is responsible for killing Jackie and my other sister. That is what Echo said."

"Not surprising. It's not true. Your mother took her own life. And as far I know, nobody knows who actually killed your other sister. Although, I'm starting to have my suspicions."

Suicide. It didn't ring true. Lilith tried to put the image of Jackie with a woman who would willingly give up her life and those two images did not mesh. Whatever Jackie was, Lilith had always seen the life in her.

"Trust me," Lucy said, seeing Lilith's doubt reflected in her eyes. "I was there. She knew it was over. For her, anyway. She destroyed herself and what we thought was her information empire until we learned differently."

"And this woman…Allison. Is it true she wanted to stop Jackie?"

"Yep. You see, Allison's mom goes way back with Jackie. And not in the good way, if you know what I mean. Allison has made it her mission to learn everything she can about Arachne, her empire and most especially her children."

"Echo said it was because she wanted to take over my mother's empire."

"Echo is a liar. But maybe a pretty convincing one. You have to trust me when I tell you that Allison is one of the good guys. Seriously. Not only does she make sure that Athena Academy continues to grow, she... well, let's just say I think she's got some other irons in the fire. That academy is an important place. It saved me and a lot of other girls. It's a home for us. For girls who are...different."

"Different?"

"Special. Talented in all kinds of ways. Even in the not-so-normal ways. You said your sister had special talents. I'm guessing she's not the only one, right?"

Lilith hesitated, but ultimately she relented. "Yes."

"You can do things? Strange things?"

"I can."

"You're not the only one, Lilith. There are others out there like you. You're not alone."

"She's not alone regardless of who is out there," Tarak said softly.

"I'm saying she would find a home at the academy. If she wanted it."

A home. Not alone. With other people like her. Lilith felt a twinge of guilt at the idea. Was it wrong to turn her back so quickly on the village that she'd called home for so many years? Yes, she'd been separate from everyone because she was part of no group, but she'd also had friends. That had been home. But what if this place could be, too?

It was all so much. The emotions bubbling inside were as overwhelming to her as the people had been back in the city. It was hard to know what she was feeling.

"You must have been watching Lilly this whole time. You knew where she was, knew her sister would come for her. You were just waiting to see what happened, weren't you? She could have been killed if she hadn't been so quick to react."

Lilith could hear the accusation in Tarak's voice as he continued to interrogate Lucy on what she knew.

"No. I promise. We were looking for her but it was just one hell of a twist of fate that you rang for help."

"Then this woman, Allison, knows that you are here. She knows that you have found me and possibly Echo?"

Lucy squinted as if she was trying to determine how to answer. "It's possible. Through a third-party person you don't need to worry about. Which brings me around to the reason we're all here. What did Echo take, Lilith? What is it you want so badly to get back?"

"A necklace," she answered.

"I hope you are kidding."

"She's not," Tarak interjected. "But it is a very special necklace with a flash drive and a tracker tucked inside it. You understand now?"

"I get it. Arachne's empire was built on information. She'd pretty much hacked into every computer system in the world. Taking pieces of people's lives. Using their darkest secrets against them. It makes sense that she wouldn't have wanted a lifetime of accumulated data to go to waste. More sense that she would give it to her children."

"Really?"

Tarak twisted in his seat and stared at Lilith. She could feel the censure in his gaze. "I thought maybe the only information on this drive was the process of how Echo and Lilith were created. You are saying there is more?"

"Hell, yes," Lucy said.

Lilith bowed her head shamefully. After what had happened between them, the way she'd opened herself to him and trusted him so completely, it wasn't right that she'd held back anything. Even if she thought she was doing it for his own good.

"I knew there was more on the drive. Files. I didn't read them all, but what I did read... Tarak, they were so horrible. When I asked you what you did you said you worked for governments. There were government leaders in those files. Names of people even I recognized. I did not think you should know about it. I did not think it would be good for you."

"No," he said carefully. "You didn't trust me with the information. I can understand that at the beginning, but you should have told me later."

"I do not suppose you will believe me when I say I forgot," Lilith said sincerely. "We have been rather busy chasing that necklace through the jungle."

"Uh-oh. Lover's spat. Look, guys, I can appreciate that relationships are tricky things. Believe me! But now is really not the time. What else did Echo tell you about the package she received from her mother?"

Lilith blinked as she tried to change focus and process the word *lover* at the same time. "Echo said she had received a gift like mine. She said there was another child. Kwan-Sook. She would have received some of this information, as well. Echo told me that this Allison Gracelyn had her killed because she wanted that information."

Lucy shook her head. "That I can promise you is not true. In fact it all makes sense. Echo got a package. She learned that two other siblings each received another third of the information and she decided she wanted it all. She tracked down Kwan-Sook and killed her. Then she went after you."

"So she has all three packages," Tarak concluded. "No wonder she was in such a hurry to get out of India. I'm furious with you now, darling, but I also congratulate you on your determination to stop her. Because of you we were able to slow her down. We actually have a chance to capture her before she has a chance to use any of that information."

Lilith tried to work out whether Tarak was really furious or only teasing. It was difficult to tell by his tone of voice. When her father had gotten angry at her it was always very easy to tell.

"Are you going to threaten to spank me again?"

Lucy erupted into immediate laughter. Tarak simply turned a few shades of red. Lilith never recalled seeing such a color on a man's cheeks.

Chapter 19

"Stop snickering," Tarak ordered his copilot.

"Sure," Lucy said. Then she snickered.

Lilith chose to ignore it. But not before a spurt of anger she recognized as jealousy emerged. Lucy was teasing Tarak. Obviously what Lilith had said about spanking was funny, although again she wasn't sure why that would be. That's when it occurred to her that Lucy and Tarak could communicate on a level Lilith and Tarak could not. Because they were friends. Because they shared the same experiences and came from the outside world.

It would no doubt always be like this when she was with Tarak and the people he knew. Once more she would be on the outside, only not because of her gift but because of how she'd grown up and where.

With a surge of determination she decided she would find a way to adjust. Tarak was worth it. Although she might be on the outside for a time in certain situations, she was sure he would always welcome her in. It was time to be part of a new world. Lilith only hoped she was ready for the challenge.

Sitting in the backseat of the cab, she felt time ticking by. Every second was an hour. Not prone to impatience, she was surprised by her behavior. But she sensed that the new life she'd just started to contemplate was only hours in front of her. Possibly minutes. She wanted to get started with it now.

"I do not understand why we are still sitting here in this lot. We could go to these key spots ourselves and search for Echo. I know what she looks like. So does Tarak. I believe that would be more efficient."

Lucy tilted her head toward Tarak. "Your girl's not patient."

"Lilly has the unique ability to carefully weigh all the options, pick the most practical course and naturally leap right in. Darling, we're waiting because once they spot Echo we want to go where she is directly. If we're at one terminal and she's at another we might miss her."

"Oh. That sounds logical."

"Thank you," Lucy said. "I try to be sometimes."

To pass time, Lilith found herself looping back to everything Lucy had said regarding Allison Gracelyn. She wondered what Jackie had done to Allison's mother and hoped it wasn't horrible. Then she thought of the school she supported. Athena Academy. "You spoke of the school for women. The academy. How did you learn about it?"

"I'm a graduate. I didn't find out about it until later in my high school career but they let me transfer in anyway, which was a great honor. I remember every day like it was yesterday. They were great years."

"And Allison built the school?"

"No, her mother started it. Allison just keeps the tradition alive. It's a place where girls are allowed to be strong, aggressive, competitive, talented, smart. It's encouraged. Girls really thrive in that kind of environment. You don't realize how much sexism still affects so many things in a patriarchal society. A woman goes for what she wants and she's labeled a bitch. A man does it and he's assertive. A woman points out her accomplishments, she's arrogant. A man does it, he's confident."

"Oh, no," Tarak groaned. "Am I going to have to leave the car for this?"

"I'll be good. I'm just letting Lilith know what kind of place it is."

Lilith thought about Sister Peter. How she might have thrived at such a school as she was all of those things and more. Maybe in her next life.

The phone sitting on the console between the two seats beeped. Lucy snatched it up. "Talk to me."

"We think we've got a visual," the voice on the other end said. "Heading for the private jet terminal. You called it."

Lilith could feel her anticipation building. Soon they

would have Echo and with so many people to help they had to be able to stop her this time.

"Got it. You know what to do. Stall until we get there."

"Out."

"Okay, let's go." Lucy pulled the car out of the lot and drove like a woman who knew exactly where she was going. Obviously she had studied the layout of the airport grounds. For a moment Lilith felt chagrined that she had doubted Lucy's plan to wait. Then once more she fell back into the side of the car as Lucy made a vicious right-angle turn and wished they had been able to walk.

"What do you mean there is a problem with my plane?"

This was not a good day, Echo decided. First she had to deal with the police at the train station, then she had to have Kent forcibly remove a driver out of his car as he had the nerve not to hand it over of his own accord. All of this was costing her time, time, time.

Now there was a man in a blue blazer with some damn airplane pin on the lapel telling her that there would be a delay in taking off because there was a problem with her plane.

They were virtually alone in the terminal. At an isolated end of the airport the company that rented the jets catered to an elite and high-paying crowd. There had been security as they entered the terminal, but as they walked the long, narrow hall to the gate, Echo could see only a smattering of staff and cleaning crew.

Large windows opened out to the rest of the airport

and she could see two white sparkling jets, one of which was about to take her home. The flight crews, consisting of two pilots and a flight attendant, had already boarded their respective planes as she could see people moving around inside both jets. A ground crew was hard at work getting them fueled and ready for takeoff.

The only person at the gate besides Echo and her men was the Indian man in the blue blazer standing behind a white counter, who was delivering some very discouraging news.

"Yes, ma'am. There is an engine light on and it must be thoroughly investigated before we allow you to take off. For your own safety, of course."

Echo tilted her head in the direction of the large windows. "There are two planes out there. Both with crews ready to go. If my plane is broken, then give me the other one. Simple."

"I am very sorry, ma'am. That plane has already been reserved. Its passengers should be here shortly."

Echo took a deep breath. She recognized that people skills were not her forte, but she also considered that in this case it might be easier to catch more bees with honey. She plastered a smile to her face and leaned on the counter in a way that she hoped signaled friendliness to Mr. Blue Blazer.

"Hear me out. You say my plane is not ready yet, but it will be shortly. However, I am here now and want to leave. Whereas the passengers for the other plane will be here shortly. Let's put me together with the plane that's ready now. And the plane that will be ready shortly with the people who will be here shortly. That would make me very happy."

The man smile and nodded. "Oh, yes, of course, but I am sorry. I cannot do that." Then he leaned over and said in a softer voice. "Big movie star is coming. Wants plane waiting for him as soon as he is ready to take off. I am under orders by my superiors to make sure that happens. But your plane will be ready very shortly. You'll see."

"Oh darn," Echo groaned.

Kent, who had been standing back with Rolf, came up behind her. "What's the problem?"

"Well," Echo whined, her shoulders dropping to a slump. "I didn't want to do this, but now I'm going to have to kill this guy." She threw up a force field around her fist and swung as hard as she could. The field out in front of her hand made impact with the man behind the counter before he was expecting it, forcing his neck back and to the right at a harsh angle. She heard it crack and then watched him drop behind his precious counter into a heap on the floor.

Walking around to where he lay sprawled out on the thin carpet, his eyes open but unseeing, she couldn't help but smile. She crouched down near his head even though she knew he could not hear her anymore.

"When I am done there will not be anyone, *anyone,* in this world who is more important than I am. Rolf, get his blazer off. Put it on and walk over to the phone near the door on the right. Tell the pilot he's to get the plane ready as soon as possible. Keep your voice low. Make like there is a bunch of static. The pilot should only see the blazer. Got it?"

Rolf did as ordered and Echo found a seat by the door. She plopped down on top of it and sighed.

It seemed like nothing was going to be easy today. Nothing.

Lucy brought the car to a screeching halt in front of the entrance to the private jet terminal. Uncaring of the man shouting at her in Hindi that she couldn't park there, she ran straight inside the building.

Tarak jumped out and waited for Lilith to extract herself from the backseat. She started to take off at a full run and realized her skirt wouldn't allow her that kind of movement.

Beautiful certainly, but not practical. Next time they went chasing after her psychotic sister, she would remind him that she needed more practical clothes.

"Tarak, wait. I cannot move in this thing."

Tarak stopped and turned around. He instantly recognized the problem and sighed, clearly disappointed that he was going to have to destroy such a beautiful piece of clothing. He knelt down in front of her and began ripping the material in front so that her legs would have the freedom to move.

"You can buy me another one and I will turn around as many times as you would like," she promised, trying to comfort him.

He looked up at her and smiled, and she returned it. Then she saw a flash of skin between the gap in the material he had created. She was glowing.

Instantly she backed away from him.

"Yes, I see," he said. "Be careful, Lilly."

She nodded and then he once more turned to follow Lucy down the terminal. This time when Lilith ran she kept up with him stride for stride, driving her legs as hard as she could. At the end of this long hall was Echo.

It was time to get her necklace back.

"Okay," Rolf said. "The pilot is preparing the plane for takeoff. We'll follow this gate down to the tarmac. They're wheeling up a set of stairs for the hatch."

Echo glanced down at the crew busy preparing the plane for flight. "Is that our luggage out there?"

Luggage was a euphemism for two carry-on bags that they had purchased to transport their guns. While they never would have made it past the terminal security checkpoints armed, the baggage check for private jets was not as stringent as a courtesy to many of the high-profile passengers who used them. The people who rented the planes asked for and received a certain amount of discretion regarding their personal belongings as long as they didn't try to carry them through the airport.

"Call down there," Echo told Rolf. "Tell them I want the bags inside the plane not in the luggage compartment underneath."

"Why?"

Echo shot him a deathly glare. "Are you seriously standing here questioning me? After the day I've had? Call down there and tell him to put the bags in the plane. Up front where I can get to them. We need to be prepared for anything."

"Yes, Echo."

Without further questions, Rolf actually headed down to the tarmac to instruct the ground crew directly. Two more men in orange blazers met him at the doorway as he made his case. Echo watched as the stairs were rolled up to the sleek jet's door. Someone from inside the plane released the hatch and one of the workmen tossed the bag inside.

Then Rolf gave her a thumbs-up as if it was time to board.

"Kent, let's go. It's time to leave."

"Yeah, in a second. I need to hit the can."

He wandered off into the bathroom marked for men, and Echo nearly screamed with frustration. Tempted to leave him there, if only she didn't have to kill him, Echo walked over to the door that would lead her outside and opened it.

"Any year now, Kent!"

There was no response from across the hall. Determined that she would pull him out of the bathroom in midstream if she had to she started to walk toward the men's room when she stopped.

Her senses went on high alert. Glancing around, there

was only her and the dead body in the gate. What in the hell was causing…

"Hold it right there!"

Echo glanced down the hallway and saw a tall red-headed woman running at high speed. She could care less about her. It was the man and the woman in the blue sari who was currently outpacing him that drew her attention.

"Kent! Get out here now!"

Reaching for her gun, she growled when she recalled she was unarmed. Just then the bathroom door swung open. And Kent walked out with two hands over his head. The man behind him was holding a gun.

No, nothing was going right today.

Lilith pulled up short, as did Lucy and Tarak. Lucy's man had successfully detained one of Echo's men, his security credentials allowing him to carry his weapon inside the terminal.

"Our two guys on the ground should have the other one by now."

Tarak walked over to the window and nodded. "He's on the ground, his hands over his head. Good work. Your men know what they're doing, Lucy. Not that I would have expected anything else."

"I only work with the best."

Lilith ignored the chatter, however, and kept her eyes trained on Echo. The woman didn't appear to be concerned about her fate. Only mildly irritated. Walking toward her, Lilith pulled at the glove. Loosening it until it released its grip on her hand. She dropped the first glove and then went to work on the second. By the time she dropped both of them, she was standing only two feet away from Echo. She knew there was no point in getting any closer. The field would have already been constructed around her.

"I want my necklace back."

Echo reached inside her vest and pulled out the gold spider, letting it dangle from her fingertips. "You mean this necklace? Hmm, no."

"You cannot win. We have your men. You are trapped. Give me the necklace and you will not die."

Echo merely smiled. "I'm not going to die anyway. If you want the necklace why don't you take it?"

Quickly Lilith reached out to snatch it away, but as she suspected her hand bounced off whatever it was that Echo used to separate herself from the rest of the world. "You can't touch me. You can't shoot me. You can't have the necklace. It seems like what we have here is a stalemate."

"We can't shoot you," Tarak corrected. "But your men are not so invulnerable. How difficult would it be for you to watch us blow off their kneecaps?"

Echo leaned forward clutching her stomach as she laughed. "Not very difficult. Especially since I was going to kill them myself as soon as I was on the plane."

"You bitch!" Kent moved as if to strike at her, but the man behind him stopped his actions by jamming the gun farther into his spine.

"Sorry doll face. You had your uses, but I wasn't about to leave anyone alive who knew that Lilith existed. But I guess the cat is out of the bag now." Echo turned back to Tarak. "Anyway, you're welcome to torture them if you think that might help. But I sincerely doubt it."

Slowly Echo started to take a step toward the door. Then another.

"How do you think this can end?" Lilith asked.

"It's going to end with me getting on that plane," Echo told her. She turned and bolted for the door that led down to the ground. The man who had been holding the gun on Kent changed his direction and fired at her, only to watch the bullet bounce off.

"Stop!" Tarak shouted. "There is no way to tell what direction the bullet will ricochet. Call down to the pilot. He's got to disable the plane. Now."

Lilith, however, wasn't listening. She hadn't come this far only to let Echo slip out of her grasp. She immediately followed Echo through the door and down the steps. Another door led outside and she could see that the men holding Rolf were suddenly unsure about what to do.

"Echo," Rolf called out. "Help me!"

"Sorry, Rolf, honey. You're on your own." Echo raced for the stairs that led to the plane. She climbed them two at a time, but when she reached the top step she saw that the flight attendant, a small woman wearing another blue blazer, was attempting to close the hatch on her.

"Close that door and it is the last thing you'll ever

do." Echo put her leg inside the plane, preventing the woman from shutting the hatch completely. Then she grabbed the flight attendant by the collar and shoved her hard toward the cockpit. "Tell the pilot to start the engines now. Tell him either he gets this plane off the ground in the next five seconds or you all die."

Lilith heard Echo's shouts and listened as the engines came to life. Desperate, she chased up the stairs after her but she could see Echo pushing the staircase away from the plane with all her strength. The sudden jerk underneath Lilith had her falling forward and she was forced hold on to the steps with both hands. She started to crawl the rest of the way.

"You just will not give up!" In order to get more leverage, Echo got on her knees and shoved at the staircase until there was at least a foot of space between the plane and Lilith. Then she leaned out farther and gave it another shove. The momentum of the staircase on wheels carried it back another foot.

Lilith held on and quickly scrambled for the top. "I will have that necklace."

"You'll have nothing! It should have been mine, anyway. All of it. You meant nothing to her. Nothing."

"Then why did she visit me?" Lilith challenged. "Why did she come to see me instead of you? Because she knew deep in her heart that I was her favorite!"

Rage transformed Echo's face into something impossibly ugly. "You'll pay for that. You will pay!"

But just as the words fell from her lips, shots started

to rain down from above. Lilith covered her head and watched as Echo had to refocus her energy. She was still on her knees inside the hatch but her arms were outside of the plane.

Lilith knew that she was concentrating on forming her force field and making sure she was covered from above. Lucy's man must have shot his way through the glass window to be firing at her from such a position.

The necklace dangled from Echo's neck. It looked vulnerable to Lilith.

One chance, she thought. Once chance now while Echo was distracted.

More shots were fired and she could hear Echo scream as she worked to deflect the bullets. Lilith got into a crouching position on the stairs. The timing would need to be perfect.

One, two and then she jumped. Off the steps and into the space between her and the plane. Her hand reached out and grabbed the gold spider, clasping it as if it were a lifeline. It cut into her hand painfully, but that only made Lilith more determined to hold it. Echo's head dropped as the necklace pulled around her neck.

"Damn you!" She grunted even as Lilith's weight began to pull her out of the plane. Lilith held on with two hands and looked up into her sister's face, now red from strain as well as fury. If she could just reach up and touch her it would be over, but as soon as she had the thought the gold chain snapped.

Lilith felt herself falling and then her feet hit the

ground hard. The jolt shot through her ankles and knees. Pain poured through her whole body as she tried to roll backward and disperse the energy. Her head hit the ground hard.

She lay on her back motionless. There was a ringing in her ears. She wasn't sure if that was from the roar of the engines or the shrieking that must have been coming out of Echo's open mouth.

She tightened her grip around the spider and lifted it so she could see it. Bringing her other hand up, she slid the back open and saw the flash drive tucked securely inside.

Then she looked up at the plane and saw that Echo had already shut the hatch. The plane started rolling forward and she had no doubt that the pilots had no choice but to comply. Echo could be very convincing.

She was going to get away.

"Lilith! Lilith!" Tarak scrambled down to where she was still lying flat on the black tarmac.

"I have it," she whispered, trying to show him what was in her hand.

"Lilly, you need to listen to me. You need to retract the poison. Now. I'm going to have to touch you. To check for injuries. Do you understand?"

His face was a little fuzzy and it was still hard to hear him over the ringing. Ringing that she didn't understand at all now that the sound of the plane was becoming more distant.

"She's getting away."

"We can't stop that. She's got a gun to the pilot's

head. That doesn't matter, though. None of it. Just tell me you can retract the poison so I can see where you're hurt. Please, Lilly. I have to be able to touch you."

She understood.

If Tarak wanted to touch her then she would not allow him to be hurt. She closed her eyes and concentrated on letting the fear and the anger and the urgency she'd felt recede.

"You can touch me now," she told him even as she lifted her empty hand to his cheek. "You can always touch me."

Then his face dimmed. She felt the light start to fade around her. Her eyes closed and there was just the ringing. Then nothing.

Then blackness.

Chapter 20

"I want to make sure you are up for this."

"I keep telling you I am all right."

"You keep me telling me, but I will believe it a little better when you are off your crutches."

Lilith smiled seductively. "I am not on my crutches now."

Tarak stared at the woman on the bed and smiled. His wife. It was quite hard to believe and sometimes so utterly easy it took his breath away.

It had been a whirlwind of experiences since they lost Echo. Lilly had fallen exactly eight feet three inches when she leaped from the staircase to make a grab for Echo's necklace. The fact that she'd caught it and it suspended her fall momentarily, allowing her to get her feet under her, probably spared her even more injury.

As it was, she was left with a severely sprained ankle, a bruised foot and a minor concussion. He'd been forced to take her to a hospital for X-rays but when it was confirmed that nothing was broken, he'd whisked her away. There was no point in arousing any sort of suspicion regarding her condition and given that she didn't have complete control of her mental faculties he thought it best that she recuperate in private.

He'd taken her to a resort facility north of the city he'd discovered years before. Out of New Delhi, away from people, where she could have peace and he could think about his next move.

Lucy had followed Tarak to the hospital and had initially demanded the necklace. She said she would personally hand it over to Allison Gracelyn, who was truly the only person to be trusted with the information on the flash drive, but Tarak had resisted.

It was Lilly's necklace. It was hers to give—or not give—to whomever she wanted. He hadn't been prepared to take that decision out of her hands while she was unable to speak for herself.

Lucy eventually relented, but did tell him that she would be reporting back to her superior, who no doubt would share the entire story with Gracelyn. Tarak was fine with that. He had a strong feeling that when Lilly did come around, she might be very curious to meet Allison Gracelyn.

It was only days after her fall, while she was resting in bed and he was feeding her soup and thinking how happy he was to have a solid roof over his head, that he popped the question.

Actually it had been more like a statement. He explained that she was going to be his wife.

Tarak smiled as he recalled her shocked expression. Her eyes had widened and she started to shake her head. But he simply kissed her. And kissed her again. Then one more time until she relented. He asked her then if she wanted to marry any other man, to which she was forced to say she would never want another man to touch her the way he touched her.

And so he told her she was stuck with him as a husband.

After a small, intimate ceremony, Tarak quickly saw to arranging some very legal paperwork with the help of some government contacts. It seemed his wife had the perfect idea for a place to start their honeymoon.

"My dear, are you trying to seduce me? Again? I fear you have become downright scandalous," Tarak teased.

They were in the honeymoon suite of one of the finest hotels in Phoenix, not too far from the White Tank Mountains, beyond which was situated the Athena Academy. Lilith was lying back in bed wearing nothing more than a pink silk slip. Not unlike what she'd been wearing the night she first asked for his help. Only this time it was not her obligation to wear it but her choice.

Her ankle was still wrapped securely, but Tarak had found many ways to give his wife as much pleasure as

possible without jostling her too much. In fact one of
her favorite words was now *more*. He was a very happily
married man.

He walked over to the bed and dropped the towel he'd
only recently wrapped around his waist after having
taken his shower. He'd just left her side, but he couldn't
resist the lure of her. His hand rested on her tummy and
he enjoyed the feel of silk warmed by skin under his
palm. Bending down, he kissed her. She had become
quite a student of lovemaking in the last few weeks, and
what she lacked in experience she more than made up
for with enthusiasm.

Yes, he was a very happy man indeed.

"We're supposed to be getting ready for your big
meeting," he told her even as his hand moved from her
stomach to capture her breast. She sighed and let her head
fall back into the pillow, clearly wallowing in his touch.

"We will. Soon. But this time is ours, yes? For a
little while."

"For as long as you want it," Tarak said.

She gazed at him then with her serious expression. He
found it to be her most popular. He was always working
on pulling other ones from her. A smile. A laugh. Even
a pout. A devilish gleam. But it was slow going. His
Lilly was just learning to live in so many ways.

But every time he made her chuckle uncontrollably,
which he found he could do if he touched her in exactly
the right spot underneath her ribs, he felt like a god.

She reached up to touch his face. "Is that true? For

as long as we want? I know eventually you must go back to your work. I told you once I didn't want you to. The thought of you being in another jungle, this time without me, makes me nervous."

"No doubt. Who would save me from the occasional stray tiger?"

"I am serious. I will worry. But I realize that I was wrong. I cannot tell you what to do. Especially when I know what evil there is in the world. That you stop people like Echo. Plus, she's still out there."

Tarak rolled onto his back but he reached for her hand so that they were still connected. "When I left Columbia I wasn't sure I ever wanted to go back. The problem isn't the danger. Not really. And sometimes yes, you can make a difference with the work. But I find it becomes harder and harder these days to know who to trust. I started on a quest to find my parents' murderers. I continued on because I could think of nothing else to do with my life. That has changed. I have something to do with my life now. I have you."

"You will miss it. You will resent me."

Again, he turned to face her. "Never. This isn't your choice, darling. This is mine. I promise."

She smiled softly and it made his heart soar. Then she bit her lip.

"What is it?"

"It occurred to me that if you do not work and I do not work, we will have a very difficult time getting on in this world without money."

Tarak couldn't control the burst of laughter that erupted from his belly. "Ever my practical little flower. Trust me. I would not have us destitute. I told you my father was English."

"Yes."

"Well, he was very English. The Hammer-Smith family goes way back, you see, with many titles and all sorts of property to go with them. Trust me when I tell you we will not starve. In fact, when we are done here I want to take you there. I want to show you my estate. The land there is very different from India. The temperature will be colder than you are used to. And the rain…well, let's just say it rains a lot. But there is a beauty to it that you will appreciate I am sure."

"And then?"

"Then we pick out where we want to live. What we want to do. You have thought about it."

She nodded. "I have. I want to be close to a place of science. I thought I was cursed for all of my life, but now I understand it is neither a curse nor a gift. It is simply what I am. It is my responsibility to learn everything I can about what I can do. If I can use this for good I will. I must."

"That definitely sounds like plan. Good. I like the way you're thinking. Then let's get you up and dressed so we can have our little meeting and then get on with the business of our honeymoon."

"Tarak." He was about to roll off the bed when she stopped him with her hand. He gazed down at her face and was sad to see that the smile was gone, once more replaced by her very serious expression.

"Yes?"

"I do not know if it is possible. I have not stopped to consider such things. But you mentioned your family. Your lineage. If I do get pregnant…if I had a baby…"

"We would be blessed," he said, caressing her cheek.

"What if she was like me?" she whispered, her voice tight with fear.

"Then I would be doubly blessed."

The view was spectacular, Lilith thought as she drove toward the mountains. She'd never seen anything quite like this. The size of the sky was impossible. It was as if they were surrounded by blue. Only the stark outline of the mountains seemed to interfere. And the land. The land that seemed to go on forever, so flat with colors like she'd never seen before. Not brown. Not orange. Not gold. She felt so far away from her village in India that she couldn't imagine that these two places could actually exist on the same planet.

Tarak drove the rented Land Rover over a narrow road called Script Pass. Eventually the road wound down into a valley at the base of the mountains. There Lilith got her first sight of the Academy.

Tarak parked the Rover in front of the main building and got out. He circled the car and opened the door, prepared to help Lilith gently to the ground.

"Do you think it was all right to wear jeans?"

They had quickly become her new favorite piece of clothing. While she knew her husband was partial to saris—he bought her a dozen to replace the one that he'd ripped—Lilith preferred the freedom of movement the pants gave her, especially as she still needed to negotiate the crutches.

"Given what you're about to do, I imagine no one will mind that you are in jeans." He pulled her crutches from the back of the car and handed them to her.

"You approve of what I am doing."

"I do." He nodded.

It made her glad to hear. It wouldn't have changed her mind, but knowing that she had his support was important. She navigated her way inside the building and saw that two women were already in the main foyer waiting for them. One woman was older with short gray hair and impeccably straight posture. Next to her was a younger woman of average height and shoulder-length dark hair. She wore a sophisticated cream skirt suit that made Lilith instantly regret her jeans and long T-shirt.

She imagined she would also have to explain the gloves. The kind she wore today were short. Just to her wrist. But she found she still needed them when she knew she was going to be among strangers.

"Hello," the older woman said. "And welcome to Athena Academy. I'm Christine Evans, the principal of this school, and this is Allison Gracelyn. But I'm sure you're already aware of that. You must be Lilith."

Lilith stopped and handed her crutches to Tarak. He hesitated to take them for a second, but she nodded her head. Her ankle was much stronger and her foot barely bothered her anymore. She limped forward and took the outstretched hand that Christine offered, then turned to Allison and shook her hand, as well.

"Please pardon my gloves. I wear them only as a precaution, but they make me feel more comfortable."

"No excuses necessary," Allison said politely. "Lucy, who you know is an alumna of this school, told us everything. She was sorry that she couldn't be here today but as she explained it…"

"She left a very warm bed," Tarak supplied. "I know she was anxious to return to it."

Allison coughed politely. "Yes. Anyway, she said you were very brave in going after Echo. A true sister in the Athena tradition."

Lilith shook her head. "I do not know if that is true. But Tarak says I can be very persistent."

"It's one of my favorite qualities," he said. He then shook Christine's and Allison's hands. "How do you do?"

"Very well," Allison answered. "Mr. Hammer-Smith, I can't thank you enough for providing the help that Lilith needed to track Echo through the jungle. I understand you were injured, as well."

"Minor stuff."

"And now you and Lilith are enjoying a honeymoon, I understand. Congratulations."

Lilith nodded. "Thank you. But I did not call this

meeting to discuss such things." She stopped and looked around the empty building. It was exceptionally quiet, she thought, for a school filled with girls.

"They are in class," Christine explained. "If you're wondering where the girls are. The classrooms are just down that hallway. Plus, we have several outlying buildings for different purposes. Our science and computer lab for one. Maybe you would like a tour?"

"I don't think that Lilith arranged for this meeting so that she could tour the school grounds, either, Christine." Allison stepped forward. "I came a long way to be here for this. You know that. I could ask you to trust me, but only you can make that decision."

Lilith nodded. "You stopped Jackie."

Allison nodded. "With help, I was able to uncover her information empire, yes. But you know that in the end she chose to take her own life."

"Yes. Lucy told me. And you are aware of what Echo is?"

"I have been given detailed reports."

"Reports will not be enough. You must understand that beyond her skills and her ruthlessness, she is sick. Twisted in a very dark way," Lilith insisted. "Maybe even more than Jackie was. Jackie could at least pretend…civility. I do not know that Echo has this skill."

"I understand."

Lilith reached inside the neck of the T-shirt she wore

and pulled out the gold necklace. She had only taken it off during those times when Tarak made love to her because she did not want something so dark to be part of something that was so beautiful. Beyond those times she had guarded it with her life and her poison.

Pulling it over her head, it almost seemed as if the necklace weighed a thousand pounds. "You understand that this is only a piece of it."

Allison took the ugly gold necklace from Lilith and cringed. "How very Jackie. Yes. I am aware of that. More than you know."

"The responsibility is yours now," Lilith said. "It is up to you to stop her. To find the other two packages and destroy all of the information. You will destroy it, won't you?"

"Still wondering if you can trust me?"

Lilith assessed the woman standing in front of her. The gleam of sparkling intelligence was impossible to miss, as was her internal fortitude. "No. You remind me of someone. A friend I used to know. When I heard about this school I thought she would have made an excellent student here. If you are half the woman she was, then yes, I do trust you."

"Thank you."

"Let's go, sweet. I need to get you off your feet," Tarak said.

Lilith took back her crutches. She nodded to the two

women and began to turn when she stopped and met
Allison's gaze one last time.

"You will stop her. Won't you?"

Allison returned her gaze directly. "Lilith, I promise
you. I will stop her."

* * * * *

*Don't miss the final chapter
In this Athena Force Adventure!*
Disclosure *by Nancy Holder
Available July 2008.
Turn the page for a sneak preview.*

En route to the National Security Administration
Fort Meade, Maryland

A dark, sharp wind threw autumn leaves against Allison Gracelyn's windshield as she put through her call to Morgan Rush, who was already at NSA for the emergency meeting. After the open and cloudless big sky of the Arizona desert, the frosty Maryland night grounded her in reality—her world was a lowering, stormy place; her safety zone as narrow as a grave; the situation as out-of-control as a nightmare.

No. I'm in control. I have a plan, she told herself. *I'm on my game. I can make this happen.*

She unrolled the window of her sleek black Infiniti and held out her NSA badge toward the security guard, who stepped from his kiosk to take it. The chill bit into Allison's ungloved hand. Beyond the kiosk, hidden by the night, the Men in Black patrolled the perimeter of the vast complex of the National Security Administration. The MIB were crack security forces of "Crypto City"—suited up in black riot gear, armed with submachine guns and God knew what else. Not one of them would hesitate to open fire if given the order.

She knew at least one person who would gladly give the word. Her volatile new boss, Bill McDonough, was furious with her for taking the day off with no explanation beyond the vague and unenlightening "personal business." NSA was sitting on top of a time bomb—literally—and the level of terrorist threat had shot from orange to bright red around the same time that Allison's return flight to Washington took off from the airport in Phoenix.

Coincidence? She didn't know yet. She didn't know what Echo was capable of. Lucy Karmon had described Echo's maniacal rage when she, Lucy, had completed her mission to steal the spider necklace from her. "Wacko beyond bonkers. Way beyond. I've never seen anything like it."

That same black-and-gold necklace had dangled from Allison's neck on her return flight to the East Coast, hidden from view beneath a black turtleneck sweater. Allison had complemented the sweater with black wool pleated trousers and low-heeled boots, which was good, because she hadn't had any time to change her clothes and they would work well in a meeting about preventing thousands if not hundreds of thousands if not millions of deaths.

She had flown to Phoenix specifically to retrieve the necklace from Echo's half sister, Lilith, to whom it had been bequeathed. Lilith wanted no part of the evil that came with her inheritance, while Echo had murdered men, women and children—and would have murdered Lilith—to steal Lilith's share as well as her own.

Still, a nuclear attack just didn't seem like Echo's style.

"Rush," Morgan said, the deep timber of his voice caressing her earlobe, the low, male rumble as pleasurable as running her cold hand along the warmed leather seat of her car.

"Yeah, hi, Morgan," Allison replied, adjusting her earpiece, keeping her voice neutral. Even during a national security crisis, Morgan threw her off. She had a feeling McDonough had assigned Morgan to her task force—Project Ozone—to keep an eye on her. Surely McDonough had no idea what working in close quarters with Morgan did to her insides. Or maybe he did.

"Meeting's set up in Conference Room A," Morgan said. "I ordered you a latte with soy milk and two sugars."

He remembered her beverage of choice. Any other time, she might have smiled.

"Thanks. I'm on site." Which he might already know, if he was keeping tabs on her. "I'll be up in five minutes."

"Hold on," he said. "I'm getting a red e-mail."

"Okay." Her adrenaline spiked. Red meant extremely urgent.

As she waited, she glanced at the time on her dash. It was 7:35 p.m. McDonough had called the meeting for 8:00 p.m. She'd been on the go for nearly twenty-four hours, but she could make another twelve or so before she started getting sloppy.

"We got some more," Morgan continued. He was obviously referring to the team's successful cracking of chunks of the heavily encrypted chatter between the unstable Middle Eastern nation of Berzhaan and the despotic nation of Kestonia. "Big stuff. You called it right." His voice betrayed his anxiety.

Damn it, she thought. She didn't want to be right about a probable nuclear attack somewhere on the Eastern seaboard in less than a month.

"Brief me first, my office," she told him. She wanted to walk into that meeting fully informed.

"Will do. Something else is incoming," he announced.

"I'm holding," she said. She took her badge back from the guard, who waved her on to proceed. The white Jersey gate raised and Allison rolled onto the grounds of the most heavily guarded, mysterious facility in the alphabet soup of national and international intelligence agencies.

Allison heard the gentle ping signaling an incoming text message on her handheld.

SSJ: STAY OUT. U R COMPROMISED. CALL ASAP.

An icy chill washed up her spine. SSJ was Selena Shaw Jones, CIA, whom she had sent to watch for intel at the headquarters of Oracle, the supersecret spy organization of which they were both members. Selena's choice of words was telling. Employees stayed away. Spies stayed *out.*

"Okay, here it is," Morgan began.

"Morgan, save it. I'll be there soon." She disconnected. A microsecond later, her cell phone flared to white noise. She had reached the perimeter of the NSA's new and improved jamming field. She glanced at the handheld. Selena's message had disappeared. Nothing else electronic would work, not her laptop, nor her PDA. Nothing.

"Damn it," she whispered, ticking her glance toward the central building, which rose into the night like a twinkling Rubik's Cube. Compromised how? By whom?

Echo, she thought. *She'd made her next move.*

She pulled her car over to the turnout. Her face prickled as she kept her speed slow and easy, hanging a U back to the gate. No one else was leaving, and she knew her Infiniti was a conspicuous ebony dot on several dozen surveillance cameras as she unrolled her window and stuck out her badge for the same guard who'd waved her through. She remained silent; she was a top-level NSA agent, and there was no need to explain her comings and goings unless requested.

The guard's phone—a secured landline—rang as he

took her badge. Her heart stuttered; her mind raced. Was it an order to detail her?

As he reached for the handset, she forced herself to look unconcerned. He swiped her badge and handed it back to her as he put the receiver to his ear. She left her window unrolled, on the chance that she might be able to eavesdrop. But he closed the door of the kiosk, sealing himself inside.

The Jersey gate had not yet raised.

Her gaze ticked toward the shadows, where the Men in Black patrolled. If she tried to bolt the gate, they just might shoot her.

Through the window, the guard's eyebrows raised; his forehead wrinkled as he looked at her through the window. She did not react, merely gazed placidly back at him, although her heart was trip-hammering against her ribs.

Then the barrier went up, signaling permission to leave. Her hands shook on the wheel as she drove through. She took slow, deep breaths and kept her face slack and expressionless, picking up a little speed as she neared the NSA-only on-ramp onto the Baltimore-Washington Parkway, because anyone would speed up a little. It would look odd if she didn't. She fought the urge to floor it. She wasn't safe yet. She could still be summoned back. Shot at if she didn't comply.

She eased onto the on-ramp. Traffic was relatively heavy, and fat raindrops spattered on her windshield. She moved into "dry cleaning" mode—evasive maneuvers designed to reveal a tail, putting space around her car—in case she had to gun it and get the hell out of there.

With one eye on the traffic, she reached across to the passenger seat, where her leather briefcase lay facing her. She flipped it open and slid out her laptop. Using top-secret NSA data gleaned via the Oracle system, Allison had shielded her cell phone and wireless connections from eavesdropping with state-of-the-art sophistication; she should theoretically be immune to invasion, even this close to Crypto City. She popped the lid and punched in a macro, taking her eyes off the road long enough to scan the monitor windows showing a dozen views of Storage Unit #217 at Old Alexandria Self-Storage, just two short blocks from the new Oracle headquarters. The storage unit door was still bolted; her paint cans and tarps were undisturbed. Illuminated by a tiny light she had installed inside the otherwise empty paint can, the gleaming golden spider necklace still lay inside.

I'll kill you before I let you have it, she silently promised Echo. It was a promise she fully intended to keep—even if the Eastern seaboard blew up before the month was over.

Harlequin Blaze marks new territory with its first historical novel!

For years readers have trusted the Harlequin Blaze series to entertain them with a variety of stories— Now Blaze is breaking down the final barrier— the time barrier!

Welcome to Blaze Historicals—all the sexiness you love in a Blaze novel, all the adventure of a historical romance. It's the best of both worlds!

Don't miss the first book in this exciting new miniseries:

BOUND TO PLEASE
by Hope Tarr

New laird Brianna MacLeod knows she can't protect her land or her people without a man by her side. So what else can she do—she kidnaps one! Only, she doesn't expect to find herself the one enslaved....

Available in July wherever Harlequin books are sold.

REQUEST YOUR FREE BOOKS!

2 FREE NOVELS PLUS 2 FREE GIFTS!

◈ HARLEQUIN®

INTRIGUE®

Breathtaking Romantic Suspense

YES! Please send me 2 FREE Harlequin Intrigue® novels and my 2 FREE gifts (gifts are worth about $10). After receiving them, if I don't wish to receive any more books, I can return the shipping statement marked "cancel." If I don't cancel, I will receive 6 brand-new novels every month and be billed just $4.24 per book in the U.S. or $4.99 per book in Canada, plus 25¢ shipping and handling per book and applicable taxes, if any*. That's a savings of close to 15% off the cover price! I understand that accepting the 2 free books and gifts places me under no obligation to buy anything. I can always return a shipment and cancel at any time. Even if I never buy another book from Harlequin, the two free books and gifts are mine to keep forever.

182 HDN EEZ7   382 HDN EEZK

Name	(PLEASE PRINT)	
Address		Apt. #
City	State/Prov.	Zip/Postal Code

Signature (if under 18, a parent or guardian must sign)

Mail to the Harlequin Reader Service:
IN U.S.A.: P.O. Box 1867, Buffalo, NY 14240-1867
IN CANADA: P.O. Box 609, Fort Erie, Ontario L2A 5X3

Not valid to current subscribers of Harlequin Intrigue books.

Want to try two free books from another line?
Call 1-800-873-8635 or visit www.morefreebooks.com.

* Terms and prices subject to change without notice. N.Y. residents add applicable sales tax. Canadian residents will be charged applicable provincial taxes and GST. Offer not valid in Quebec. This offer is limited to one order per household. All orders subject to approval. Credit or debit balances in a customer's account(s) may be offset by any other outstanding balance owed by or to the customer. Please allow 4 to 6 weeks for delivery. Offer available while quantities last.

Your Privacy: Harlequin is committed to protecting your privacy. Our Privacy Policy is available online at www.eHarlequin.com or upon request from the Reader Service. From time to time we make our lists of customers available to reputable third parties who may have a product or service of interest to you. If you would prefer we not share your name and address, please check here. ☐

HI08R

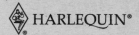

Thoroughbred *Legacy*

Launching in June 2008

A dramatic new 12-book continuity that embodies the American Dream.

Meet the Prestons, owners of Quest Stables, a successful horse-racing and breeding empire. But the lives, loves and reputations of this hardworking family are put at risk when a breeding scandal unfolds.

Flirting with Trouble

by *New York Times* bestselling author

ELIZABETH BEVARLY

Eight years ago, publicist Marnie Roberts spent seven days of bliss with Australian horse trainer Daniel Whittleson. But just as quickly, he disappeared. Now Marnie is heading to Australia to finally confront the man she's never been able to forget.

The stakes are high when it comes to love, horse racing, family secrets and broken promises.

A new exciting Harlequin continuity series coming soon!

ATHENA FORCE

Heart-pounding romance and thrilling adventure.

Allison Gracelyn is on the run from authorities and is being set up. Yet clearing her name will mean battling an adversary wielding weapons unlike any she's ever seen. Only with the help of her handsome National Security Agency contact will she be able to stop her enemy's deadly reign. But once she's up close and personal with her long-distance partner, full disclosure suddenly seems the greatest risk of all.

ATHENA FORCE

Will the women of Athena unravel Arachne's powerful web of blackmail and death... or succumb to their enemies' deadly secrets?

Look for

DISCLOSURE

by *Nancy Holder*

Available in July wherever you buy books.